CHERRY AMES, CAMP NURSE

The CHERRY AMES *Stories*

☆   ☆   ☆

The VICKI BARR *Flight Stewardess Series*

"I don't see a thing except a scratch,"
Cherry said gently

CHERRY AMES
CAMP NURSE

By

HELEN WELLS

~~~~~~

NEW YORK

GROSSET & DUNLAP

Publishers

Contents

CHERRY AMES, CAMP NURSE

CHAPTER I

Summer Begins

"I," SAID A LIGHT, CLEAR VOICE, "AM A MOUN-taineer! And I know who you are."

Cherry jumped. "Yes, I'm going to be camp nurse." She smiled at a pretty blond girl of about eleven who stood in the train aisle. "You don't look much like a mountaineer to me," she added, laughing.

"Confidentially, I'm Sue Howard, and there's the rest of the Mountaineers—my cabin mates, I mean. 'Mountaineers' is our unit name." The girl waved to a group in the seats farther up the aisle. Then she sat down beside Cherry in the temporarily vacant seat. "We're all dying to meet you, Miss Ames."

Cherry held out her hand—a cool, strong, im-maculate nurse's hand. "How do you do, Sue Howard? How did you know my name?"

"We heard about you from Aunt Bet and Uncle Bob."

1

"Oh, of course."

Aunt Bet and Uncle B. B. Wright were the directors of Camp Blue Water for girls and its brother camp, Thunder Cliff.

Cherry had met Mr. and Mrs. Wright through a neighbor when she had been at home in Hilton, Illinois, for an Easter visit with her family. The neighbor, Mrs. Pritchett, who lived three houses down the tree-shaded block, had known all four Ameses for years and could remember Cherry and Charlie in their twin baby carriage.

"Someone who likes children and who likes the outdoors," the Wrights had said, "is the kind of nurse we want," and Cherry certainly qualified. Her mother felt, and Cherry agreed, that this job would be a good change of pace from her recent nursing work in a big city department store. Besides, she'd always enjoyed working with children.

Interviews in New York followed. Dr. Robert Lowell, the camp physician, and his wife (who was a nurse herself) both approved Cherry's qualifications—and liked her. The Wrights did, too.

So here she was on the last Saturday in June, her luggage holding a summer's supply of nursing equipment and crisp white uniforms, riding into the mountains of northeastern Pennsylvania in a train jammed with lively campers.

Sue went on, "I hope you don't think I—well, sounded awfully forward, Miss Ames, speaking to you like that, but I'm an old camper, you see. So's all my cabin, except Katy Osborn. She's new." Sue's forehead wrinkled when she said Katy's name, as if she were doubtful or baffled. "I thought maybe we could be a great help to you. I mean, show you around and explain how we do things at Camp Blue Water."

"Thanks ever so much. It *would* be a help. And I'd love to meet the other Mountaineers."

"Oh, good!" Sue said. "I'll bring them over—"

As Sue left, Aunt Bet came down the aisle. She was a sympathetic young woman with a smile like a sunburst.

"Hello, Cherry, has anyone brought you sandwiches and milk yet?"

The camp director said that they just had a basket lunch on the train for the two-hundred-odd girls, their counselors, and the boys and young men counselors belonging to the boys' camp—Thunder Cliff.

"It gets too complicated to do more than that," Mrs. Wright said, "but supper at camp will make up for it. My husband went ahead with the service staff last week. They'll have everything ready for us." Aunt Bet smiled at three very small girls who were entertaining themselves by making faces. She turned back to Cherry. "Three of our Midgets. Have you met many of our girls yet?"

"I'm in the process, Mrs. Wright. They're a fine group, aren't they? I'm really looking forward to spending the summer with them."

"Wait until you see the girls in action," Aunt Bet said proudly.

"They seem to be plenty active right now," Cherry said, laughing. "I've already helped Dr. Lowell treat a skinned knee and hiccups. And, oh yes, I refereed a fast spelling bee. Loved it. I hope I'll do lots more than nursing."

"Of course you will. I think the girls are going to love you, Cherry. Anyone who looks as pretty as you do—" and Aunt Bet rose, with an extra smile for Cherry's rosy brunette good looks. A counselor at the end of the car was beckoning, and Aunt Bet went toward her.

That was the girls' head counselor, Kay Rogers, down there with Aunt Bet, Cherry remembered. She had met Kay a few days ago at the Wrights' apartment, at a staff meeting. Cherry had met most of the counselors for both camps then. She recalled that day as a friendly confusion of faces, voices, handshakes, and instructions.

A few persons had been outstanding, among them the boys' head counselor, Reed Champion. Cherry hoped to become better acquainted with the likable young man.

And now, this bright morning, a crowd of young figures flitted around her. The older girls exchanging snapshots were Seniors. The eleven-to-thirteen group, Cherry knew, were called the Intermediates, and they were the peppiest ones. Juniors—the eight to tenners—and the Midgets—the littlest ones— made up the other age groups.

"Well, here we are, Miss Ames," Sue announced, coming back up the aisle, five or six more young faces looming up behind her. "You *said* you wanted to meet the Mountaineers."

"I do! But first, I'd like you all to call me Cherry."

"Oh, thanks. We were going to, anyway, pretty

soon," Sue said. Then, changing the subject with no preliminaries at all, she asked, "Miss Ames, I mean Miss Cherry, did you ever nurse a criminal?"

"Don't go asking silly questions," said a plump little girl. "I'm Mary Alice Burton, Miss Ames, since *some* people don't perform introductions. Such as my old friend Sue."

"I'm Ding, that's short for Margery Page." This girl had cropped hair and an impish smile. "*Did* you ever nurse a criminal? We have a serious reason for asking."

Before Cherry could answer, Sue made a point of formal introductions.

"Dot and Dee Smith. They're twins, though you'd never believe it, except for looking exactly alike."

Dot and Dee had reddish hair, and were alike as two freckles. "Stale old joke," the taller twin protested.

"I have a twin brother," Cherry said with a grin, "but people can tell us apart."

Sue and Ding whooped with laughter. The Smith sisters looked delighted, and Mary Alice chuckled.

"The reason people can tell Charlie and me apart," Cherry said, deadpan, "is because my twin is blond and I'm dark."

She thought for a moment of her brother, and her parents, and their comfortable gray frame house in Hilton. Except for that very good visit with them at Easter, she'd scarcely seen her family for months. Why had she chosen to spend the summer away from them? Cherry felt a pang of homesickness.

"Why, I'm as bad as any other new camper,"

Cherry thought. That reminded her of Sue's earlier remark.

"Sue, didn't you say there's a new girl in your cabin this summer? Where's Katy?"

There was a brief silence. Then Sue said politely that perhaps Katy would decide to join them later.

"Is she in hiding? Nothing criminal, I hope," Cherry teased.

Sue was flustered. She picked up a newspaper.

"Speaking of criminals, Miss Cherry, and we were, before—would you please look at this article?"

Lil Baker, one of the counselors, called to Cherry, "Don't let my girls pester you with that newspaper story. They're mad for mysteries."

"So am I," said Cherry. "Let's see what's so interesting." As Sue handed her the newspaper, Cherry asked, "What's so special here?"

"Well, the man they suspect did it—" Sue hesitated. "A few people think they've seen him passing through the towns near our camp."

"A mystery on our own doorstep!" Cherry exclaimed.

"Could be. Please hurry up and read it, Miss Cherry," she said, pointing to a headline:

NEW CLUE IN NEW YORK LOAN COMPANY ROBBERY

As she read the news article Cherry noticed that the twins wandered away, and then Mary Alice murmured, "Excuse me," and left. Presently Ding scampered off, but Sue waited doggedly beside Cherry. So it was Sue who was the mystery hound.

"What do you think?" Sue asked.

"Let me finish the whole article first."

The case was one Cherry had read about, but now an unexpected new angle had cropped up. Two weeks ago a lone man had robbed a loan company in New York City. He had entered unobtrusively late on a rainy Friday afternoon when the loan company office was crowded. He must have known that Friday the fourteenth (the date nearest the fifteenth) was the semimonthly date on which people came to pay off their loans—a day when a great deal of cash was being received in the loan office.

The man must also have known intimately the layout of the big office, and where the employees would be busy at that hour. For he had boldly walked down a private corridor and into a deserted inside room which held the company's safe. No one saw him, no one stopped him, since the employees were occupied in the front office with clients. From the safe the man took a large sum of cash. It was only on his way out of the inside room, as he was going down the corridor, that two women employees noticed a man wearing a raincoat and a hat pulled low over his face. But when they tried to stop him— for this area was for employees only—the man pulled a gun.

"Great balls of fire!" he had said, according to the women's report, "Get in that door and keep still!"

He had pushed them into a washroom, keeping them covered, locked it, and then apparently had made his way through the crowded outer office into the street—just another man in slouch hat and rain-coat whom no one had noticed.

The curious thing was that both women had de-scribed the man as *faceless*. They had been able to see a little beneath the pulled-down hatbrim, but the face had been smoothly, horribly featureless. He was slightly below medium height, they reported, but otherwise the bulky, free-swinging raincoat hid his figure completely. The only identifying mark was the man's use of the phrase, "Great balls of fire!"

What was so provoking about the case, Cherry thought, was that the loan company would release no information about *how* the man had got into the safe, nor would they speculate on the possibility of an inside job. But now, a reporter had extracted from the loan company the fact that one of its cash-iers was a man below average height who frequently used the phrase, "Great balls of fire!" The man's name was Jack Waldron, he was twenty-eight years old, and he had left for his vacation just a few days before the robbery took place.

"It would have been easy enough for him to come back to the office, disguised like that, and take the money," Sue said. She had been watching the place where Cherry was reading.

"Easier, I guess, than to attempt the job from the inside. That is," Cherry said, *"if* he is the robber."

"He used the same funny words. Why do you suppose he did such a stupid thing?"

"He may have gotten excited when the women

discovered him, and blurted it out. Just a minute more, Sue—"

Cherry continued to read. "This reporter learned today that the cashier, Jack Waldron, has not reported back to work, although his two-week vacation period is now over. Employees of the loan company stated that Mr. Waldron had planned to go on a camping trip during his vacation. A friend who was to have accompanied him was taken sick. Mr. Waldron told his fellow employees that he would go through with his plans, anyway, even though it meant camping alone."

Sue urged Cherry to read the last paragraph.

"Friends of Jack Waldron expressed concern at his failure to report back to work. He was due back a week ago. Some feel it is possible that Waldron may be lost, or ill and alone in some woods. Others regard this as unlikely, since he is an experienced camper. A few of his friends received picture postcards from him, postmarked June 10 and June 11. (The robbery occurred on June 14, when semi-monthly payments were made.) These post cards were mailed from Lanesboro and Pleasant Mountain, small towns in northeastern Pennsylvania. No word has been received from Waldron since June 11.

"Telephone inquiries by this newspaper to these towns elicited the information that a young man who may be Waldron has been seen there. A grocery store owner recalls that the man, carrying a camper's pack on his back, made a purchase about ten days ago, about June 19 or 20, late in the evening. A hardware merchant made a similar report.

"A description of Waldron has gone out to police in this widespread area. He is about five feet six, weighs approximately 150 pounds, has brown hair, and regular features. No photograph of him is available. Friends at the loan company, where Waldron worked for six months, say that he told them he had been raised in an orphanage, served in the Army, and had been honorably discharged, then worked in various accounting firms and banks. He is unmarried and has no known relatives."

That was the end of the newspaper article. Sue had been standing on one foot and then the other, until Cherry finished reading.

"Well, what do you think?"

"It certainly sounds as if he had a bleak, lonely life," Cherry said. "Not that that would excuse an armed robbery—if he really came back to New York from Pennsylvania and did it."

"Just three hours by train. Everything points to Jack Waldron," Sue said. "Things couldn't look much worse for him, could they?"

Cherry pretended to shiver. "I hope we don't find any armed desperadoes lurking around Camp Blue Water."

"If we did," said Aunt Bet, overhearing, "we'd probably put them to work painting the dock. Get your suitcases ready, everybody! We'll be there in ten minutes!"

CHAPTER II

A Puzzling Request

BY MONDAY, CAMP BLUE WATER WAS IN FULL SWING. Everyone was busy, enjoying a swim in the lake, paying calls from cabin to cabin, and taking their first lessons in horseback riding. The arts and crafts cabin and the woodcraft area were humming with projects, and the nature counselor was in constant demand to answer questions about newly discovered plants, flowers, and animals.

Cherry had a bird's-eye view of the activity from the infirmary, which was a log cabin perched high up near the top of a slope. Looking down, Cherry could see the campers' cabins scattered among the grove of sweet-smelling spruce, pine, and hemlock trees; the Midgets' and Juniors' cabins at a safe distance from the edge of the beautiful blue lake.

Off to the east, at the camp entrance, stood the directors' "Main House" and office, and the airy Mess Hall. Then came the barnlike Playhouse where the girls would put on theatrical productions, and invite the boys from Thunder Cliff to square dances. Besides these, workshop cabins, tennis courts, and grassy play areas made up the rest of camp. At the west end of camp was the cabin which Cherry shared with five other staff girls and a mouse.

Cherry and Jean Wheeler did not mind the mouse. Since Jean Wheeler, called Nature Girl, taught nature lore and was hike leader, she had encountered many animals more frightening than a field mouse. Cherry, being a nurse, felt sympathy for all living creatures.

"I admit a mouseless cabin would be cleaner," Cherry said. "But honestly, Leona, there's no need to rip open our cots each time before climbing in."

"I wish I knew a nice, helpful cat around here," Leona sighed.

Leona Jackson was the dancing teacher, her sister Doris Jackson was camp pianist. They were high-strung, city-bred young women, not used to country living. But they were willing to laugh at their own greenness. The other two occupants of this roomy cabin were Ruth M. who supervised arts and crafts, and Ruth J. who was the head swimming instructor.

Cherry saw less of her cabin mates than of little Sue Howard, whose "Mountaineers" cabin was just across the path. Sue ran over before breakfast to say good morning.

She was prompt to acquaint Cherry with Blue Water ways. "You'd better not spread out any clothes to dry in this field, Miss Cherry," she said early one morning. "I've seen squirrels come out of the woods and scamper all over the things we leave around."

"Thanks, Sue." Cherry gazed into the dense woods which rose like a wall behind the field. "How deep is this forest?"

"I don't know," Sue answered, "but it's big. On the other side of it is Thunder Cliff." Sue pointed out the footpath along the edge of Long Lake which led to the boys' camp.

"How long is Long Lake?"

"Gosh, at least five miles, maybe farther. They say the far end is wild and deserted. We're not allowed to row near there, or go exploring or hiking there."

"Even with counselors?"

"Even with counselors, and Jean Wheeler leading the hike. Especially not to Tall Man's Island."

The name arrested Cherry's attention.

But Sue was already telling her about the Eplers' farm nearby, where the camp purchased its eggs and butter. "The Eplers are an awfully nice young couple," she said enthusiastically. A little farther away, she added, was another farm, the Model Farm, where the campers had their own vegetable patches and helped take care of the farm animals. Last year Sue's cabin had been in charge of raising a calf.

"I can hardly wait to see her grown up into a cow," Sue said. "Will you come with us, Miss Cherry? Please?"

"I'd love to, but it depends on when I'll have time off from the infirmary."

Cherry was very busy these first days helping

Dr. Lowell and his wife organize the infirmary. The log cabin was divided into a clinic, a small examining room, a supply room, and a large room holding four cots. "A complete little medical unit, although I'd rather not attempt surgery here," said Robert Lowell. For any serious emergencies, he told Cherry, they would rely on the hospital in Martinsville, the nearest good-sized town. The doctor said it was a first-rate hospital.

"We don't really expect any serious cases," Janet Lowell told Cherry. "When Bob and I first came up here, four summers ago, we were all set for appendicitis and a broken arm or leg. But the Blue Water girls fooled us."

"You don't sound a bit sorry," Cherry said, smiling.

She liked the young, brown-haired Lowells—Robert so quiet, and Jan so gay, both of them such responsible, warmhearted medical people. It was pleasant to have another nurse here to work with. Cherry and Jan wore crisp white uniforms and caps. Dr. Robert, as the children called him, wore starchy white, too.

"Nursing won't monopolize all your time," the Lowells told Cherry. Jan taught the girls fine needlework when she had spare time, and the doctor was always willing to give a first-aid lesson on the infirmary's porch. "Bob and Bet Wright may ask what you'd like to do, Cherry, so think about it."

The infirmary's first patient was the new girl from Sue's cabin. Katy Osborn came limping in on Tuesday morning, all by herself.

"Why, where's your counselor?" Cherry asked. "Didn't she or some of the other girls offer to bring you up here?"

"I didn't tell them I was coming. They'd have laughed at me," Katy said. She limped over to a bench and dropped down. A pretty little girl with fine skin and silky hair, Katy wore the simple camp uniform of shirt and shorts with an air. "Besides, I don't want the other girls to be fussing around me. Oh, my ankle!"

"That's a shame," Cherry said. "Let me see it."

"Can't the doctor see it?" Katy murmured. "If you don't mind—"

Cherry looked at her in surprise. "He will, in just a minute." She explained that Dr. Lowell and his wife were busy setting up health-record forms for each girl, and this morning it was Cherry's job to be the receiving department. She examined Katy's ankle.

"I don't see a thing except a scratch," Cherry said.

"But it hurts! Can't the doctor—please?—"

Dr. Lowell came in and examined Katy's ankle. He, too, found nothing wrong with it except a scratch.

"But that's exactly what hurts," Katy said pleadingly. "Quite a lot."

"I'll paint it with iodine," Dr. Lowell reassured her. "Then you can run along and enjoy yourself."

After the doctor had applied iodine and a Band-aid, and had left, Katy continued to sit forlornly on the bench.

"Homesick?" Cherry asked.

"Oh, no," Katy said. "It's nice at Blue Water. It's just that I don't see any fun in tennis practice. The other girls work so hard to win, it's so silly."

Perhaps this girl with her air of being specially privileged did not like to compete with better players. But it was only tennis *practice* . . . Cherry wondered.

"Besides, I couldn't play tennis with this bad ankle."

"Now, really, Katy, there's nothing the matter with you. I'm sure you have enough spirit to overlook a scratch."

Katy looked as if she wanted to cry but was too proud to. "Why can't anyone around here see how hard it is, especially for a new girl, Miss—Miss—?"

Cherry supplied her name, and said encouragingly, "New ways aren't easy at first, are they? Do you want to tell me what's bothering you?"

Katy burst forth into an account of her troubles. She was obliged to make her own bed and help sweep out the cabin—before she'd had breakfast, at that! . . . Well, yes, so did all the other girls. But she wasn't used to it, she'd never had to do such things at home. Besides, if she wanted a shower, she had to walk way over to a shower cabin for it. That was how she'd scratched her ankle, on a stone along the way.

"Poor Katy," said Cherry. She felt amused, but concerned for the youngster, too. "But, you see, part of the fun at camp is living mostly outdoors, living very simply. And doing your share of the chores together with your friends is part of the fun, too."

"Sue and the rest aren't my friends," Katy said very low.

"Do *you* like them?"

"I'm trying to."

Katy stood up, excused herself, and limped down the hill. From the way her shoulders drooped, it appeared that she felt infinitely sorry for herself.

Yet Cherry liked this pretty girl. She was anxious to hear more about Katy from the camp director, in his crowded office, when she delivered the day's medical report to him.

"Just read this letter from Katy's parents," Bob Wright said. He was a lean, homely, likable man. "Next they'll write me they don't want their treasure to go swimming for fear she'll get wet. Katy is a nice girl or she could be, if her parents ever let her stand on her own feet."

From the letter it was clear that Katy, an only child, had had everything done for her. Overprotected, indulged, cradled in luxury from babyhood —no wonder she was frightened, indignant about making her bed, and lost among the other campers.

"Maybe she'll learn at camp, this summer," Uncle Bob said. He peered at Cherry through his round glasses like a kindly owl. "We'll all do everything we can to help her."

"I'll try, too," Cherry promised. Maybe she could drop a hint to the Mountaineers of Katy's cabin.

Then Uncle Bob surprised her. "You know what I think? And Lil Baker thinks, too? The girls themselves are going to be the ones who help Katy.

They'll either cure or kill her. That cabin is going to have a summer they won't forget."

The Lowells were right, Cherry did have a pleasant amount of free time. Of course she remained on camp premises within call of the infirmary, and she was not idle. Whenever she saw a way to make herself useful, she joined in. It was fun to lend a hand with the Midgets, at their cabin called the Beehive, in honor of Bea, their unit counselor. Two afternoons Cherry helped the swimming staff with the kindergartners in the crib. The craft shop attracted Cherry, as the girls collected reeds to weave baskets, and some started leather work. Cherry thought about what sort of contribution she could make.

"You probably know a good deal about biology, since you're a nurse," Aunt Bet said that first week. "Perhaps you'd like to help out in the nature department."

"We might start a Can-You-Name-This Shelf," Cherry suggested, and Aunt Bet agreed that that would be a good idea.

At first, though, Cherry was content to do the small extra jobs that no one else had time for. That was how she happened to bump into Reed Champion, and to meet the Eplers.

Sophie, the cook, announced one morning that she needed extra cream and eggs at once, for ice cream and cake for Ding's birthday. (It was a Blue Water custom to hold a birthday party for any girl lucky enough to possess a July or August birth date.)

Who would go over to the Eplers' farm for extra supplies? Cherry volunteered.

"Our station wagon is temperamental," Uncle Bob told her, giving her the keys. "It'd be surer to walk over to the Eplers'—it's only fifteen minutes' walk—except that you'd have to carry the eggs and cream on the way back, and it takes a lot of eggs and cream to make enough dessert for this gang."

Cherry didn't expect the motor to stall on so short a drive, but it did. She was considering leaving the car in the road and continuing on foot when a twin station wagon came toward her. It stopped.

"Stuck?" the young driver inquired cheerfully. "Need help? I'm the head counselor at Thunder Cliff, remember?"

"Of course I remember," Cherry said, "and even though this motor has me confused."

Reed Champion laughed, and slid out from behind his own wheel. He was tall, athletic, already sunburned, and moved with an easy strength. He lifted the hood and released a part of the mechanism.

"She always catches like that with a new driver," Reed said. "You're all right now—ah—I'm awfully sorry but I can't remember your name except that it's some kind of a fruit." He actually blushed.

"It's Cherry, but sometimes I think Tutti-Frutti would be easier for people to remember."

"Tutti for short? Anyway, the name Cherry matches your coloring." Then Reed Champion looked downright embarrassed. He changed the subject. "Is this your first season in camp work?"

They talked camp for a few minutes, in the warm sun, with green trees blowing gently around them. Reed was dedicated to his work with young people, Cherry could see. In the winters he taught physical education and coached basketball and baseball at a Long Island high school. Every summer, except for an enlistment period in the Air Force, he had been first a camper, then a junior counselor, and now head counselor at Thunder Cliff.

"The kids say you can tell an old-timer by how long he's known old Reed." The young man smiled, a wide, friendly smile. "A lot of us love this mountaintop. We come up here Thanksgiving and Easter, to hike and sort of keep an eye on the camps. Fred and Vernie Epler invite us to dinner and tell us the local news."

"I'm on my way to the Eplers' now," said Cherry. She remembered about the waiting cook, and explained to Reed Champion.

"Well, I won't detain you," he said. He started to walk back to his own car, then he stopped. "See you around. If you're ever free for an evening drive—or on your day off—?"

"My hours aren't definite yet, but it would be nice to see you." She was surprised, because Reed obviously was no ladies' man, but pleased too that he had asked her for a date.

Reed shook his head as he climbed back into his car. "I'm so busy that if I make appointments ahead, usually I have to break them at the last minute. Anyway, I'll look forward to seeing you on Saturday evenings. The boys visit the girl campers for a square dance on Saturdays." He waved. "Give my regards to the Eplers."

The Eplers' house stood at the entrance to a small working farm. Cherry liked the neat, bright look of the place, with its well-tended rows of garden produce, the freshly painted barn, and the rolling green fields beyond. It was nearly noon, and appetizing odors floated from the house.

Cherry tapped at the screen door. No one came; she heard the clatter of dishes, and a radio newscast. She knocked again, several times, but when no one answered, Cherry walked to the the back of the house and went to the open kitchen door. Two young men and a young woman were having lunch there and listening to the news.

"Hello?" Cherry said. "Anyone at home to a Blue Water caller?"

To her surprise, the yellow-haired young man jumped from his chair, and went hurriedly out of the room.

The other two people looked anxiously at each other. Then the remaining man nodded, and the young woman rose, turned off the radio, and came to the door.

"Come in, miss. I'm Vernie Epler." She and her husband wore blue denim work clothes. She gave Cherry a friendly, if strained smile. "Always glad to see Blue Water folks."

"Please don't let me disturb you," Cherry said. "I'm interrupting your lunch. Please go ahead."

"Not a bit of it," said Fred Epler. He pulled up

a chair for her. Vernie offered her a cup of coffee. "Afraid we don't know your name," the young farmer said.

Cherry introduced herself. "I'm new here. I've already heard about *you*, though, from the children."

The Eplers smiled. "The campers are one of the nicest things in our neighborhood. That Reed Champion—now there's one fine boy," Fred said.

Cherry nodded. "This looks like one fine farm, too. Have you been here a long time?" For although she was here on an errand, the Eplers received her as a neighbor, and expected her to be as friendly as they were.

Fred Epler told her that he and Vernie had been here about three years, ever since Fred had inherited the farm from a great-uncle.

"But we feel as if we'd always lived here. Belong to the church, and the Grange, and put this run-down farm in good order, and Vernie won a blue ribbon for her peach preserves at the County Fair."

Fred Epler spoke with well-earned pride for both of them.

Yes, Cherry thought, they must work hard, from sunup to sundown, on their tidy farm.

Fred and Vernie were so young and devoted, they seemed almost like honeymooners. Cherry wondered about the young man who had left the room so abruptly—she had not heard of any third person at the Eplers'. She noticed that Vernie and then Fred glanced into the other room.

"I hope I didn't drive away your—ah—" Cherry hesitated. "The other young man."

"Our friend," said Vernie. "Not a local boy. Fred's— A friend of Fred's. They haven't seen each other for a long time." She seemed under some necessity to explain.

"I guess you think it's funny," Fred Epler said to Cherry, "the way he bolted, hey? Mac's tired. He hasn't had much sleep. I guess that's why he —well, maybe didn't think he was fit for company."

"I'm not company," Cherry said, "and honestly you don't owe me any explanations."

But Fred Epler insisted Mac had to come in and be introduced. He went into the other room. Cherry heard them talking. Then the two young men returned together.

For a moment Cherry had a passing impression that Fred and his friend looked somewhat alike. But she dismissed it. For one thing, their coloring was entirely different—Mac was yellow-haired and he wore a small mustache. He seemed worn, though not much older than Epler. Like Fred and Vernie, he was windburned and sunburned.

"This is Mac Cook, Cherry Ames." Fred gave the young man a slight push forward. "Tell the young lady you're a little bit girl-shy."

Mac Cook did seem shy, or at least ill at ease. He said hello courteously to Cherry, and apologized for walking out. Otherwise he had nothing to say.

Cherry thought he was an extremely amiable-looking person, who looked as if he could be fun, but she wondered why he seemed so tense. The atmosphere in the farm kitchen grew strained.

"Well, I—I came for some extra cream and eggs," Cherry said to fill the uncomfortable silence.

Just as she started to follow Vernie outdoors, toward the springhouse, Mac Cook barely touched her sleeve.

"Will you do me a favor?" he asked.

"Depends on what the favor is," she replied.

"It isn't much," he said anxiously. She saw signs of fatigue around his eyes. "I—I—well, I'm not feeling very good—and the neighbors around here, if you don't visit them right away, think you're being unfriendly. So would you mind," Mac Cook said all in a rush, "not mentioning to anybody that you've seen me here?"

Cherry looked for some guidance toward Fred Epler, but he was lighting a pipe. Vernie was waiting outdoors, half turned away; Cherry could not see her face. They must have heard Mac Cook's request. If it were wrong, certainly people like the young Eplers would not be party to it.

"All right," Cherry said, still puzzled. "All right, if you wish."

His relief was visible.

She purchased the eggs and cream, and drove the short distance back to camp. "It still seems a bit queer," she thought, "but after all I'm a stranger here. The Eplers know how things are done, and I don't, so I'll just be a Roman and 'do as the Romans do.'"

CHAPTER III

P.E.P. Stands for Purdy

CHERRY BELIEVED SHE WAS ACQUAINTED BY now, the second week of camp, with practically everyone in and around Camp Blue Water. During the commotion of Fourth of July, she had met dozens of campers of all ages. She now had all the coun·selors sorted out by name, including Ted and Jimmy Sims who taught riding and sailing. These two young men lived at the Main House, along with the camp directors and Dr. and Mrs. Lowell. Cherry had even improved her acquaintance with Sophie, the cook, and her helper and the elderly handyman around the place.

"You haven't met the horses," Sue Howard pointed out, on one of her before-breakfast visits to Cherry's cabin. "I guess you haven't met Mr. Purdy and his wonderful barn, either."

"How can you meet a barn?" Cherry teased her.

"This barn is different. It's stuffed with all kinds

25

of costumes and props and gorgeous draperies. Mr. Purdy lets us borrow them for our camp shows."

Sue explained that Mr. Purdy was a commercial photographer, who lived in a summer cottage nearby, and these intriguing items were things he would not need for a while, or had no space for, at his studio in New York City. Sue thought he also stored old negatives, out-of-use cameras, bulbs, and such things in his barn.

"Well, why haven't I met this fascinating character?" Cherry demanded.

"Because he just got here yesterday, from the city," Sue said. "Ding and Mary Alice and I saw him yesterday, opening his cottage for the summer. I guess it's Mr. Purdy's vacation. He said hello to us and invited everybody over to eat apples off his trees. He's a funny little man. I mean, he's lots of fun."

Sue's report was accurate. Cherry met Mr. Purdy that afternoon, while taking a wildflower-picking stroll with Lil Baker and the inmates of the Tumble Inn cabin, the Dingdong Belles, and the Mountaineers—all Intermediates. It was fortunate that Cherry had worn a sturdy cotton blouse and skirt and not her white uniform, for all of them were grass-stained and muddy, and bedecked with daisy wreaths on their heads.

"We must be a sight to behold," Lil remarked to Cherry as they straggled back toward camp.

"Hold it!" a squeaky voice commanded. A little man trotted toward them. "A close-up, please, ladies!"

He was a funny little man, with a beret perched
on his nearly bald head, garish sports clothes, and
rope-soled sandals on his feet. He seemed to be
enchanted with the flower maidens, and nearly fell
off a jutting rock trying to snap them at "an interesting angle."

"Enough, enough!" Lil Baker protested. "How
are you, Mr. Purdy? It's nice to see you again this
summer."

He let his camera swing from its strap around
his neck, and scrambled down to them, beaming.

"Miss Lilian! Are these grown-up young ladies
the same *children* I saw last summer? Hello, twins"
—he nodded to the redheaded Smiths—"and I remember Ding and Sue, and—and all of you, naturally."

The girls giggled. Katy stepped forward as if, being so pretty, she were eager for the photographer to
notice her. Mr. Purdy went on chatting with them
all impartially.

"Are you going to stage *Macbeth* this summer,
or is it the *Follies*? Did you receive the snapshots
I mailed you last winter?"

"Oh, yes, Mr. Purdy, and Uncle Bob used a lot
of them in the camp catalogue," Sue said.

"I can act," said Katy, but she was drowned out.

"Will you lend us costumes and props again this
summer, Mr. Purdy? Will you come to see us?"

The little man said "Yes, yes, yes!" to everything.
Lil Baker raised her voice to introduce Cherry.

"A new nurse—well, that is fine," said Mr. Purdy,

shaking hands with her. "So you are new here. Really I am not such an old settler, either. I've had my cottage only two years."

All of them strolled down the road, in the direction of camp, to see his place. It was the nearest of all the neighbors' houses to Blue Water. Cherry found it smaller and shabbier than she had expected, judging by Mr. Purdy's rather high-flown manner. It was just a modest two-room cottage, backed by a ramshackle barn and some apple trees.

"Your house needs a coat of paint, Mr. Purdy," said matter-of-fact Mary Alice.

"Yes, yes, but I'm not sure it would be worth the trouble," he said airily. "Or the expense."

"Mr. Purdy," said Sue, "we have a bet about your first name. None of us know what it is."

"Now tell me, Sue, do you like *your* name? . . . Not very well? . . . Well, I don't care much for mine," the little man said. "It's Paul. And my middle name—may my dear mother be forgiven—is Ethelbert."

The girls found that fairly awful. Then Sue exclaimed, "But your three initials spell Pep! That's fun."

"Exactly. Very quick of you. And do you know, I use the name Pep as my trade name? That's what I sign on my photographs. In the city many of my friends call me Pep or Peppy."

Cherry thought the name suited him. Especially when he stood on tiptoe and vigorously shook an apple tree, so that they could carry refreshments back to camp with them.

The girls were serious when they asked Mr. Purdy for costumes and props, Cherry learned. Sounds floated up to the infirmary from the Playhouse—sounds of home-grown vaudeville acts in rehearsal. Sue confided to her that one skit was called "Fussy Flossie at Blue Water," and could Cherry guess who was meant?

"I hope that you're not being unkind to Katy," Cherry said.

"It's Katy who's being unkind to—to— Well, our whole cabin can hardly believe it! She begged to adopt a kitten from that nice Mr. and Mrs. Clemence, who own the Model Farm. A gray kitten with a dear little face. Then Katy brought the poor little thing home and forgot to feed it regularly. Didn't even bring it fresh water!" Sue said indignantly. "Said that it could catch Miss Leona's mouse. And it's only a baby, still wobbly on its paws. All the rest of our cabin is taking care of the kitten. Katy says she forgets. Forgets! It sleeps on my cot now."

Cherry suggested that Katy's lack of any sense of responsibility was not her fault—it was the way she had been brought up.

"But Katy will have to learn, or she'll be in trouble," Cherry said. "Why, the Midgets do better than that."

The six- seven- and eight-year-olds were busy with a project of raising baby ducklings. A dozen yellow balls of fluff floated at the Midgets' share of the waterfront and swam tamely in to shore to eat grain out of outstretched palms.

The camp was alive with numerous projects. Indirectly Cherry learned of some of them. Via Sally Trent's skinned knees, she heard about the older girls' trip to one of the lake coves, in search of specimens for their plant collection. From three girls' upset stomachs, the Lowells and Cherry found out about Sophie's good-natured permission to make fudge the previous afternoon when it rained. A scorched thumb was testimony of what the girls were doing at the woodcraft center, under Jean Wheeler's supervision. This especially interested Cherry, and she went down the hill to see.

The point was, the girls were preparing themselves for overnight hiking trips. The other side of the mountains called to them, and the flowery opposite shore of Long Lake seemed to beckon. Cherry found girls of various ages working seriously with saplings, cut in the forest, fashioning them into lean-to shelters and crude dish racks. She watched Jean Wheeler show one group how to use a fireplace "—sometimes we'll use the camp shelters and fireplaces along the way—" and showed samples of what kind of woods were best for cooking.

"Cherry, you look wistful." Jean Wheeler laughed at her.

"If you'd have me, I'd love to come along sometime on an overnight hike," Cherry said.

"You're cordially invited, Nurse, *provided* you can pass tests for outdoor skills. Every girl has to, before she starts out."

"I'm rusty," Cherry admitted. "Mind if I hang around and brush up?"

She made it her business to work with Katy, whose delicate fingers were unused to bending a sapling.

"I think this is silly," Katy said under her breath.

"Silly to know how to take care of yourself? Never mind a scraped finger. You really have a knack with wood, I think," Cherry encouraged her.

The girl gave Cherry a look of surprise and hope. "I thought you told me in the infirmary the other day that I'm spoiled. You sort of hinted it."

"No one has to *stay* spoiled and helpless," Cherry said cheerfully. She held two pieces of wood in place for Katy to join. "How's your kitten?"

"Oh, I guess she's Sue Howard's kitten now."

Katy Osborn had much to learn. Cherry hoped she would not insist on learning the hard way. She had an inkling that Katy, defiant or not, was not happy about not fitting in and would *like* to change.

"It isn't easy to discover one's own good and bad points," Cherry remarked to Katy on the morning a crowd of them drove over to the Model Farm. "Look at me, I *know* I wouldn't know what to say to a pig or a calf. Do you think I can learn?"

Katy smiled faintly. "I s'pose it depends on whether the pig and calf co-operate."

"Good for you," Cherry thought. *"At least you've found out that there is such a thing as co-operation."*

The Model Farm was well equipped. Elderly Mr. and Mrs. Clemence, who operated it as a hobby with the help of several men, left a place open on the farm schedule every summer for the children to take part. The Clemences always had plenty of time to show a girl—or a boy, on the boys' days—how to look after the animals or grow a garden. Cherry's eyes opened wide at the campers' skill. No one hurried, enjoying the warm sun and the warm, fragrant earth.

Bea's Beehive, little as they were, took care of a pen of chickens, scattering corn, while other little girls carefully gathered the eggs. Sue's cabin and rival cabins plunged with hoes and rakes into the truck garden, which had a thriving vegetable patch for each group of girls. Cherry pitched in, too, mostly to give Katy a hand and engage her interest.

Aunt Bet had said, "See what *you* can do with her, Cherry. Lil can't, and I can't do much." Katy was behaving fairly well, so Cherry stole away for a few minutes to see the older girls' project. The Seniors cultivated a large flower garden, the most striking Cherry had ever seen, with variegated blooms massed in whites, pinks, and blues. The all-blue garden with its delphinium, hydrangea, larkspur, and bachelor buttons was Cherry's favorite.

"It's a favorite New England garden," old Mrs. Clemence told her. "This July sun is helping the flowers so much, isn't it? But you look puzzled, my dear?"

"I was wondering, Mrs. Clemence," said Cherry, "whether you could tell me the exact species or horticultural names of the blue flowers. My mother is an enthusiastic gardener, she'd love to know about good, healthy strains."

"Certainly. We have a little greenhouse. If you want to walk over there, you'll find shelves of seed envelopes. Those will give you the information you want, I'm sure. They're for sale, if you care to choose any."

Cherry thanked Mrs. Clemence and walked over to the greenhouse, which stood by itself. Entering, she took a deep breath of its moist, scented air. Right at the door she found the shelves with the seed envelopes and a seed catalogue. But first, she could not resist having a look down the greenhouse's long green aisle.

A young man was watering some of the plants. Didn't she recognize that yellow thatch of hair? Wasn't that figure, rather short and of wiry build, Mac Cook? Then he turned around and Cherry saw the mustache and his startled face.

"Hello, Mr. Cook," she said. "I certainly am surprised to see you here."

He wet his lips and tried to smile. "I guess it doesn't square with asking you to keep quiet about me being in the neighborhood, does it?" He looked unhappy. "Well, by now I've said hello to most of the neighbors. Remember I told you about that?"

"So you're working here now," Cherry said. "I rather thought you had a job or business or farm elsewhere."

Mac hesitated. "Well, I'm between jobs, so to speak. This isn't my regular work. You know how it is, when you need money and take a temporary job—gosh, I'm not saying what I mean." He smiled at Cherry, for the first time, as if asking for understanding. "Summer jobs—it's good to work around a farm, outdoors. I've been bottled up all winter.

It's a good change to live and work at the Clemences' farm."

"You live here now, too?" Cherry asked curiously.

"Why—why, sure. Why shouldn't I move to where I'm working?"

"Except," Cherry thought, "that the Eplers' place is nearby, and you said you were here to visit them."

"I was sort of in Vernie's way," Mac said, as if sensitive to Cherry's thoughts. "Oh, they invited me to stay, but I didn't want to wear out my welcome, so I moved."

Mac said he had come over to the Model Farm the day before yesterday, Wednesday, after asking Fred Epler where he could get a job and lodging. And here he was.

Cherry didn't know just what to think of this story, or of Mac Cook himself. Was he one of those men who drift aimlessly from job to job, from town to town? Farm owners did hire extra hands who came and went with the summer. Yet Mac Cook did not look like a wanderer. Cherry sensed something purposeful in him. He was likable, all right—nice-looking, self-respecting and—well, the sort of person you'd expect would be lighthearted, full of jokes and laughter. It baffled Cherry that he seemed tense and watchful.

In fact, Mac was listening hard to voices outside, voices approaching the greenhouse.

"Who's that coming, Miss Cherry?"

"It sounds like Mr. Clemence and another man. Why?"

"Oh, nothing, nothing."

Then he turned and Cherry saw his startled face

Cherry went to the door of the greenhouse, aware that Mac was watching from the end of the aisle.

"Hello, Miss Ames!" The photographer doffed his beret to her. "We meet again. How are you today?"

Cherry murmured a reply, and was introduced to Mr. Clemence. She turned around to see why Mac Cook was so quiet. He had disappeared. The trowel and box of fertilizer he had been working with were gone, too.

Old Mr. Clemence did not notice; he was busy with Mr. Purdy. The photographer wished to buy some perennials or bushes, to plant around his cottage.

"Nothing expensive, please. What would you recommend?"

Mr. Clemence, as white-haired and gentle as his wife, showed Purdy the catalogue for perennials. The two men discussed rhododendron versus mountain laurel for a few minutes. Where had Mac gone to, and why? Cherry waited, pretending to admire rows of tender plants.

"Now if you want to select bushes, Mr. Purdy," said the old man, "I'll show you what we grow over in the nursery. If you'll come along, sir—"

It was several minutes after they left before Mac Cook reappeared from another aisle, with trowel and box under his arm, and carrying a hose in his free hand.

"Hi," said Cherry. "Are you playing hide-and-seek?"

"You still here?" Mac Cook was flustered. "You

mean *me,* playing hide-and-seek? Why, I went to find a hose and special nozzle."

"I'm not trying to quiz you," Cherry said pleasantly. "If you want to avoid Paul Purdy, that's up to you."

"I'm not avoiding— Who? What name did you say?"

Cherry stared at him. "Mr. Purdy, the photographer. You seemed to know him."

"Er—I did know a photographer, but not by that name."

"This one's name is Paul Ethelbert Purdy. Quite a name."

"His initials spell Pep," Mac mused.

"That's right. He uses Pep as his trade name, or professional name."

Mac Cook screwed the spray nozzle onto the hose, peering at it and adjusting it until it was just right.

"If you don't mind my asking, does the photographer live around here?"

That was no secret. Cherry told him about Purdy's cottage, close to Camp Blue Water. Mac Cook listened quietly. Then he asked:

"When did Pep—Mr. Purdy—come to his cottage?"

"Early this week. You certainly are asking a lot of questions, Mr. Cook."

"Sorry. Just curious. Why don't you call me Mac?"

"Is that because you're going to ask me for a favor again?"

Mac Cook grinned. "Well, if you don't mention

seeing me to Purdy, I'd be just as well satisfied."

The tone of voice was casual, but Cherry saw his fingers tremble.

"I didn't intend to go and tell him. But why? And won't he find out from someone else?"

Mac Cook shrugged. The moment of tension had passed. Cherry saw his rate of breathing change, the slow deep breaths of relief.

Mac Cook genially refused to say another word about the photographer. He offered Cherry a rose. She accepted it, and let their odd conversation end there, in mid-air.

Cherry went back to the seed shelf and started to choose some packets for her mother, but her mind kept going back to Mac, and the more she thought about the incident, the more puzzled she grew. Had Mac ducked when Purdy came in, or had he really gone for the hose? And why, in either case, had he bothered to carry the trowel and box back and forth?

"On the other hand I may be imagining things," Cherry half decided. "Mac moved in order to get a job. He may not have dodged Purdy at all."

"*Or maybe it's not imagination,*" cautioned another part of her mind. What disturbed her most was, why had Mac's fingers shaken? Why had *Mac* been so disturbed?

With her hands full of seed packets, Cherry started out to find Mrs. Clemence, and met her coming in.

"I'd like to buy these, Mrs. Clemence," she said, "to send to my mother."

"I'm sure she'll enjoy them," the little old lady replied. "But here, dear, let me wrap them in a package for you. You'll be dropping them all over, carrying them loose like that."

She reached for a pile of old newspapers such as country florists keep on hand for wrapping plants and cut flowers. As she pulled the sheet toward her, Cherry's eye was caught by a headline on the page beneath.

NEW CLUE IN NEW YORK LOAN COMPANY ROBBERY

It was the article she had read on the train.

Instantly, certain facts flashed through her mind: The suspected thief had gone to Pennsylvania; he was twenty-eight years old; he was rather short and of medium build.

Instantly also, she thought of Mac: *He* was in Pennsylvania; *he* could be about twenty-eight; *he* was rather short and of medium build! He had asked her not to mention his presence to anyone. His hands had trembled as though in agitation. He had disappeared when Mr. Purdy came in.

"Could he,"—Cherry's thoughts clamored— "could he be the thief?"

CHAPTER IV

A Dance and a Scare

EARLY THAT SATURDAY EVENING THE GIRLS OF Camp Blue Water welcomed the boys of Thunder Cliff to the summer's first square dance. Everybody was scrubbed till he or she shone. Reed Champion drove in with a truckload of the smallest boys.

It was still daylight at seven o'clock, with long tree shadows stretching across the camp. The Mess Hall, which had been cleared for the Midgets' square dance, echoed merrily with music from the phonograph and many pairs of scuffling feet.

In the Playhouse, where Cherry helped the counselors serve lemonade and cookies at the refreshment table, the older campers danced and bowed to each other to the accompaniment of two fiddles. The cries of old Tom Hawkins, the local "caller," sent them all whirling.

"Cha-a-ange partners! Choose your lady—" Everyone scrambled. "Docey-do to the right! Docey-do to the left! Swing your partner, and—a— Fiddle louder there, boys!"

Cherry admired the youngsters' ease in these complicated steps and figures. Katy Osborn flew by, one of the best dancers, light-footed and in a gay peasant skirt and blouse. Sue Howard was dancing and arguing with a boy of her own age and height, who wore steel-rimmed glasses and looked like a future scientist, even while bobbing around.

Sue pulled him out of the dancing circle, over to meet Cherry.

"Miss Cherry, this is D. V. Howard, my cousin and oldest friend. Here she is, D. V., the one I told you about."

"How do you do, D. V.?" said Cherry. "I hope Sue told you something favorable about me."

D. V. shook hands and looked Cherry firmly in the eye. "Sue says you're but good. You know how inaccurately she talks—that means she likes you. Have you gone on an overnight hike yet?"

Cherry was a little startled at D. V.'s bluntness—rather like Sue's. "Not yet. But I hope to."

"Well, we boys are building a new shelter along the old lake-front trail. You watch for it. It'll be solid enough for a person to live in all summer if he wanted, too. We built several shelters, other summers."

"I'll look for them," Cherry promised. "What was the odd name of an island you told me about, Sue? The place that's out of bounds."

"Tall Man's Island," Sue said. "There's all sorts of mysterious stories about it."

D. V. scoffed. "Nothing over there but snakes and swamps. That's why it's dangerous," he declared. "Say, don't you hear a game starting? You had enough dancing, Sue?"

Sue said no, but her eyes lighted up with interest. Jean Wheeler was organizing a game of softball outdoors.

"Please excuse us, Miss Cherry, while there's still daylight to play by?"

The square dance continued, and Cherry stuck by her post at the lemonade table. Several girls and their partners came over to speak to her, and she danced a few rounds with Dr. Lowell and Uncle Bob. At one point she had Reed Champion for a partner.

He hunted her up between dances, when everyone was taking time out to catch his breath and admire the moonrise.

"Care to come outdoors, Cherry? There's a good breeze off the lake. Always cool up here in the mountains, in the evenings. How are you getting on?"

"I'm having as fine a time as the campers, thanks. And I've enjoyed meeting a number of Thunder Cliff boys this evening."

Reed chuckled. "They're behaving so politely this evening that I don't recognize them."

Reed and Cherry talked about the camps, and about the surrounding countryside. Cherry asked whether D. V.'s description of Tall Man's Island, or Sue's hints, was truer.

"I guess the truth falls somewhere in between,"

Reed said. "Are you interested in seeing the island? I've been over a couple of times. It's picturesque, all right." He thought, then said, "If the counselors of both camps can get enough free time—it's a long trip back and forth to the island—we could paddle over and have a picnic supper. Then we'd have moonlight to come home. A big party of us."

"Sounds nice," Cherry said. "What are you looking so amused about?"

"We did all go over, a few summers ago, with Bob and Bet Wright acting as chaperones. That's the time when Rob and Jan Lowell got engaged. Moonlight on the lake, and stuff. I was just thinking"— Reed smiled broadly at her—"that it'd be only fair to make Rob and Jan be the chaperones the next time."

"You'd probably make them feel ninety years old."

"Well, isn't it only poetic justice?"

Reed was so friendly and so easy to talk to that Cherry wondered whether she might ask him another question. For Mac Cook's strange behavior had stayed in her mind. She asked Reed whether he knew Mac Cook.

"The new young fellow? Yes, I met him at the Model Farm."

"What do you think of him?"

"Seems all right. The Clemences wouldn't hire him if they didn't think so, too."

Cherry decided to say nothing further about Mac right now.

Reed had to see Uncle Bob at the Main House, and Cherry drifted in to the Midgets' dance, to see whether she could lend a hand there. The guests were mostly yawning. Bea White was rounding up the Midgets, to tuck them into bed. She smiled her gentle smile as Cherry picked up one little girl who had fallen asleep in the middle of eating a cookie.

"I saw you and Reed together," Bea whispered above the Midgets' heads. "Is this going to be a romance?"

"Why, we're hardly acquainted, Bea. You can't tease me *yet*."

"Watch out for the moonlight."

That was the second time this evening she had been cautioned about the moonlight. Cherry mused about that after the dance was over, and Blue Water was quiet once more. Well, Reed was very pleasant and the summer was just beginning. On the other hand, Reed was exceedingly busy heading up the boys' camp. Beyond that, she refused to think about the possibility of a romance, moonlight or not.

Two days afterward, Cherry had a bad scare. Dr. Lowell was away getting some extra supplies, expecting to be back by noon. Janet Lowell was busy down at Firefly cabin; one of the children had severely twisted her ankle and Jan did not want her to walk on it. Cherry was in charge of the infirmary when a counselor brought in Sally, an Intermediate of twelve, still in her pajamas and slippers. Sally's heavy eyes and flushed face clearly said illness.

"Sally woke up with a headache and sore throat," her worried counselor told Cherry.

"And my stomach feels sick," Sally complained.

"Well, we'll make you comfortable in bed," Cherry said, "and have you feeling well again in no time."

The counselor, Amy Clark, looked questioningly at Cherry when she helped Sally into the cot in the examining room, instead of putting her into the four-cot ward.

"Isolation?" her lips formed the word soundlessly.

"Private room," Cherry said cheerfully. That was to encourage Sally. It was too soon to know whether this was a communicable disease or not. At this stage the symptons could point to any one of a number of illnesses.

"Let's take your temperature, Sally. That should tell us something interesting," Cherry said.

It did. The thermometer read 100.4 degrees.

Cherry cleaned the thermometer, and washed her hands.

She motioned to the counselor to follow her into the clinic room. Out of Sally's hearing, Cherry asked whether any of the other girls in Sally's cabin felt ill, what Sally had been eating, whether she had caught cold.

Amy Clark answered that the rest of the girls felt all right—so far—and that Sally had been in good condition until this morning.

"Is there anything I can do here, Cherry? If not, I'd better go to my basket-weaving class. They're waiting for me."

"Yes, go right ahead. But will you send someone to tell Jan Lowell that as soon as she has strapped that ankle, I'd like her to come here?"

Jan did not come for quite a while. While she kept up a cheerful front for Sally, and put a cool compress on her burning forehead, Cherry thought busily. If this turned out to be something contagious not only every girl in Sally's cabin but every girl in camp would have to be carefully checked over and watched. Considering that the boys' camp had come visiting on Saturday night, the same precautions would have to be taken for the boys. Of course, even if Sally had influenza, as Cherry half suspected, that would not necessarily mean the others would catch it. Sally could be kept in quarantine or, safer still, sent to the hospital.

Jan came in. She listened to Cherry's brief report and looked at the TPR. Then she peeked into Sally's private room.

"Asleep," Jan whispered.

She watched Cherry get out a pail for Sally's soiled dishes, disinfectant, paper towels, a gown, and a separate hand-washing unit—just in case quarantine might be necessary.

"I wish Rob were here," Jan said. "I don't think we should wait for him though, so I believe I'll telephone Dr. Edwards at Martinsville and ask if he can come right over."

The physician drove over at once. Aunt Bet, also notified by phone, came up the hill to hear what Dr. Edwards would say. The two nurses came out on the porch and shooed her away.

"We don't want you getting this, if it proves to be contagious," Jan said. "We'll keep you informed. Please don't worry."

"How can I *not* worry!" Aunt Bet said, but she went obediently back down the slope and leaned against a tree. "Here I am and here I stay," she said, half to herself. "I'll catch Dr. Edwards on his way out."

Dr. Edwards, assisted by Cherry, gave Sally a quick, thorough examination. Her temperature had gone down a little.

"Keep her in bed, keep checking her temperature. Liquids only," the doctor said. "We can't be sure yet. Either Rob or I should see her a little later in the day."

Dr. Edwards left after the nurses promised to call him a second time if necessary.

Cherry went to the Mess Hall at noon and brought back fresh fruit juice for Sally, and sandwiches for Jan and herself. Jan, meantime, bathed Sally's hands and face, and asked questions. Sally admitted to sampling everybody's packages from home, and having played games in a damp bathing suit, although her counselor had told her to change into dry clothes. The two nurses looked at each other with a cautious hope.

"Could be grippe," Jan said, out of Sally's hearing.

Dr. Lowell arrived at half-past one, dusty and mildly annoyed.

"Had a flat tire," he explained. He listened to the nurses' report. "Any discharges from her throat? Is she sneezing?"

Sally's nose was running, but that was all so far. Dr. Lowell looked her over.

"My croaking sounds better now," Sally said with a grin.

Jan kept watch through the afternoon. Sally had all the air, liquids, and sleep that one girl could manage. When she woke up, Jan asked where she had been last Saturday, on Friday, and on Thursday, for if she had been exposed to some disease it might take three or four days for the infection to develop.

"I'm hungry," said Sally. "I wasn't anywhere except to the Model Farm and the Eplers' farm and Mr. Purdy's orchard. Same as the other girls. Say, I'm *awfully* hungry."

"What did you do at the Model Farm, Sally?" Jan asked, ignoring Sally's plea for food.

Sally giggled. "I was hoeing, racing the others, and I fell in the brook. That nice Mac Cook fished me out. I dried out pretty fast in the hot sun, but it felt awfully cold for a while."

At ten that evening, Cherry, having napped, reported for night duty. She was equipped with a warm sweater, flashlight, and a book to help her keep awake.

Sally slept soundly. When Cherry wakened her for a moment at midnight to check her temperature, she dropped right back to sleep again. It was a long night in the moonlit cabin, a long vigil.

The next day Cherry was able to tell Dr. Lowell that no nausea had developed, no rash, no vomiting. On that basis Dr. Lowell decided not to send Sally to the hospital, but to keep her under observation here.

"I'm hungry," Sally insisted. "I feel like I could

eat a huge steak!" and she indignantly sat up in bed.

"Do you mean to say," Cherry teased her, "that I've stayed up all night with a practically perfectly healthy would-be steak-eater?"

Two more days of careful, patient watching followed; two more days of bed rest and treatment for a deep-seated cold infection, and then Sally was discharged into Amy Clark's care. The symptoms which *might* have meant an epidemic in camp fortunately turned out to be only a bad scare.

"Seem like an anticlimax?" the young doctor said to his wife and Cherry.

But they all knew better than that. Without good medical care, Sally's cold could have developed into pneumonia or flu. The victories a nurse and doctor hoped most for were over illnesses which they never let happen in the first place—not a particularly showy victory, but a satisfying one.

~~~~~~

CHAPTER V

The Second Move

THERE WAS A SURPRISE IN STORE FOR CHERRY. SHE was coming along one of the wooded paths, on her way to the Main House for mail, when she saw a familiar-looking figure. It was a man with a thatch of yellow hair, and he was strewing gravel on a slippery part of the path. Cherry hesitated, went ahead—and found herself face to face with Mac Cook.

"Hello!" Cherry exclaimed. "I thought you were working at the Model Farm."

He glanced at her and uncomfortably turned away, pretending to be very busy. Was he remembering their encounter in the greenhouse? His hair and mustache seemed yellower than ever in a shaft of sunlight.

"Don't you recognize me?" Cherry asked.

"Sure. You're the nurse. Hi." He would just as soon she had not seen him, judging by his perfunctory manner, Cherry thought.

50

"I've been so busy at the infirmary, I didn't know you were working here, Mac," Cherry said curiously.

"Yes, I—I can earn a little more here than at the Model Farm. Been working at Camp Blue Water since Wednesday."

This was Friday, July nineteenth. Just last Saturday she had met Mac at the Model Farm. And the week before, she had surprised him at the Eplers' house.

"You certainly move around," Cherry remarked.

"No, I don't," Mac Cook defended himself. "I'm still living at the Clemences'. They're nice people. Said I can sleep there if I want to."

He gave her such a sharp look that Cherry did not venture to ask further questions. Well, Cherry said to herself, the camp director probably knew what he was doing when he hired this young man. But why had Mac Cook moved twice in barely three weeks? All the vague suspicion she felt about him grew stronger at discovering him on home territory. But Cherry realized that if she hoped to learn anything about Mac Cook, she would have to keep on friendly terms with him.

"I hope you'll enjoy working here," Cherry said. "Isn't this a lovely spot here beside the lake? I guess all this farming country is pretty nice. By the way, how are your friends, the Eplers?"

"The Eplers? I haven't seen them."

Cherry was perplexed. Earlier Mac had said that he came to this neighborhood especially to visit Fred and Vernie Epler. Then he had told her that

he felt he'd got in Vernie's way. Now he said he
hadn't even seen them. Had Mac Cook and the
Eplers quarreled? Not that it was her business . . .

Mac surprised Cherry by asking, "How's Pep?
Have you seen him?"

"Who?" She knew perfectly well whom he meant.

"The photographer. Paul Purdy. Pep for short.
The man from New York," he explained elaborately.

"No, I haven't seen him this week." It was on
the tip of Cherry's tongue to ask, "Have you?"

"I suppose he drops into camp now and then,
seeing that he lives so near?"

"I'm too new here to know," Cherry said.

He had prompted her last time, too, for information about Purdy. Cherry did not like it. She
must have stiffened or frowned, for Mac Cook said:

"If you're thinking that I'm curious about Purdy,
it's only because I—I'm interested in photography.
It's my hobby, sort of."

"Oh, really? What kind of camera do you have?"
Cherry challenged him.

"I— It's with my clothes at the Model Farm.
Show it to you sometime. It's—ah—it's broken now,
though."

Cherry said gently, "You're a poor liar, Mac
Cook. If you want to find out something, why don't
you ask in a straightforward way?"

"I don't know what you're talking about."

But Mac flushed to the roots of his yellow hair.
In self-betrayal? Or in anger? If this man were dangerous, Cherry did not want to rouse his anger.

She made a pleasant remark or two, and went on her way.

Mac Cook continued to work unobtrusively at the camp. Everyone except Cherry seemed to take his presence for granted. It was true that the old handyman needed a young helper like Mac. And the children did like him. Cherry saw Mac Cook whittling whistles for the Midgets. Sue Howard reported that Mac had found them a fine stand of reeds, for their basket-weaving project. He was seen putting down his hammer to climb a tree and retrieve a badly aimed basketball. In just a few days Mac Cook had made himself a favorite among the young campers.

Yet Cherry noticed something which troubled her. Mac, she could observe from the hilltop infirmary, did not walk out of camp until evening shadows had gathered, although his work and supper were surely finished earlier. Why? Did he stay around because he was lonely? Or did he prefer to walk back to the Model Farm, past Purdy's cottage, past the Epler farm, under cover of twilight? He came to work very early in the mornings, too, before most of the neighborhood was stirring.

Still, her suspicions wavered—even remembering that newspaper story—when she saw Mac good-naturedly working outside the Playhouse with the kids. He was hammering at some kind of wooden contraption, amid a group of excited girls. Sue Howard ran over to tell Cherry the news.

"We're going to put on a vaudeville show! Mac's

helping us make the scenery. He builds it, and we paint it. Will you come to our show, Cherry?"

"I wouldn't miss it for anything. When is opening night?"

"Or matinee," Sue said. "Probably a week from this Sunday, or sooner, some weekday, if we can get ready sooner. Leona Jackson says our dance routines are ready. The comedy skits are easy—we mostly write 'em ourselves, and Aunt Bet rehearses us, two, three times—that's plenty."

At the moment Mac was making a gate "for the milkmaid song and dance," Sue explained rapidly. She described an Indian skit with feather headdresses and blankets (off their cots), and a Shakespearean spoof, and a rag-doll dance with orange crepe-paper wigs which were being made right now at the arts and crafts cabin.

"We're going to do a funny infirmary number, too," Sue said. "Have you any idea where we could borrow a nurse's uniform?"

"I have a faint idea." Cherry grinned back at Sue. "But how will you make Indian headdresses and Shakespearean costumes on such short notice?"

"Oh, we'll borrow them from Mr. Purdy. He has old Romeo and Juliet costumes in his barn, and yards of draperies, even backdrops and all shapes of chairs—*everything*. Mr. Purdy's barn is a regular treasure house."

Yes, Cherry recalled, she had heard earlier that the commercial photographer stored in his barn the props and costumes which he did not currently use.

Leona Jackson told Cherry that he was generous about letting the campers borrow these things.

Sounds of rehearsal—voices, laughter, piano music, dancing feet—floated from the barn for the next few days. Cherry dropped in to watch Wednesday noon.

Mac was in the wings, disguising a small wagon with a pile of twigs, propping cardboard flames atop—a campfire for the Indian number. On the stage eight girls danced a loose-jointed routine. Katy Osborn stood in a corner mumbling and gesturing to herself.

Cherry caught Katy's eye and smiled. The girl came over.

"Miss Cherry, will you hear me say my lines? Everyone else is too busy."

Katy went into her slight spoof of Juliet's lovely lines. She was pretty enough to play Juliet, and had an unexpected sense of timing and humor. It wasn't what she said but how she said it.

"You're awfully good at this," Cherry said when Katy had finished.

"Thank you. Leona Jackson and Aunt Bet think so, too," Katy said. "The other girls won't admit it. They're jealous of me."

"Really jealous?" Cherry said. "I wonder about that. We all want to be friends here."

"Yes, they are jealous," Katy insisted. "Every girl wants to be Juliet, you know. They call me uppity and unfriendly."

Cherry detected real hurt in Katy's voice, though

she suspected any indications of unfriendliness were Katy's own fault.

"Well, why don't you show the other girls that you *are* friendly? It's so easy."

Katy looked uncertain. "How? What do I do?"

Cherry felt sorry for this youngster. Imagine not knowing how to be friends! It was as if Katy had not yet learned how to walk.

"Why not do something for the other girls?" Cherry suggested. "Something no one else remembers to do, which would be nice or of benefit to all of you."

Katy thought. "The outside of our cabin looks awfully plain. When Nature Girl took us exploring in the woods the other day, I saw some big lacy ferns and I wished we— Is it a lot of work to dig up ferns and plant them around a cabin, Miss Cherry? They'd grow, wouldn't they?"

"Yes, they should grow nicely. It's work, of course, but not much if you ask Sue and Mary Alice and Ding and the Smith twins to join you."

Katy's pretty face changed. "But you said, something *I* should do for the others, to show I'm willing to be friends."

Katy, it seemed, was not yet ready to join in with others. Very well, one step at a time, Cherry decided, then asked whether Katy knew of anything considerate she could do.

"Mmmm. It's not very Julietlike or important or anything. There aren't any closets in our cabin, our clothes get all scrambled. I could ask Mac for extra hooks or nails, and hang things up." Katy giggled.

"The other girls will think I'm crazy when they see me doing it."

"No, they'll appreciate your thoughtfulness," Cherry encouraged her. "And why not ask Lil Baker about all of you transplanting the ferns? It's such an attractive idea."

Katy nodded vaguely, thinking.

"How's that darling little gray kitten of yours?"

"I *do* remember to feed it now, Miss Cherry—honestly."

Katy wandered off to rehearse some more by herself. On the stage Aunt Bet was calling Mac. Cherry pricked up her ears.

"Anybody see Mac in the wings? Or backstage? He was here just a moment ago." Aunt Bet scrambled down across the footlights, to join Leona Jackson at the piano. "Mac would go off somewhere just when we need a man to pick up that floor screen at Mr. Purdy's. He *knows* I want him to get that screen."

"Mac's been perfectly obliging with me," Cherry heard Leona Jackson say. "He made two trips to the Eplers' yesterday to locate a milking stool for us." She began to talk to Aunt Bet about the music arrangements.

Interesting, Cherry thought. Did this mean that Mac was willing to visit the Eplers but not Purdy? Unless his going off just now was coincidence.

Later that day she learned from the talkative old handyman, who came up to the infirmary to have a splinter removed from his thumb, that Mac did not go to Purdy's place. Reed Champion had driven over to Blue Water on an errand and, having the truck, picked up the screen for Aunt Bet.

"Mac's pretty busy," Cherry said, as she put a final application of iodine on the old man's thumb.

"Yep, Mac's been busy repairin' them extra foldin' seats for the show, all afternoon. Wish he'd clear out the tool shed. It sure needs doin'."

The next day at noon Mac was helping out again at the Playhouse when Cherry strolled in. Mac apologized about not going for the screen, but Aunt Bet said it really didn't matter, he was so full of good ideas.

"If you don't mind my butting in, I have another show idea," Mac said modestly.

"Let's hear it," Aunt Bet and Leona Jackson said in unison.

Cherry wondered what those two young women would say if they knew that Mac had not wanted to be discovered at the Eplers' house—and, seemingly, had not wanted Purdy to see him at the Clemences' Model Farm. It was a curious circumstance that she was the one person in camp who had observed these incidents. Should she report them to Aunt Bet? Pretty incomplete information to report. Mac always seemed, as now, nervously aware of her presence, even though she was perched on the farthest window sill.

"Well, what's your idea, Mac?" Aunt Bet asked him. "Stop pulling at your mustache and tell us, please."

"I—I was at the arts and crafts cabin just now," Mac said, "and say, some of the girls there are sketching pictures, pretty good, too. Some of the others—" He glanced toward Cherry. "Some of the girls take candid-camera snapshots. That's some people's hobby. Well, I saw these pictures and snaps and—well—"

"You thought, 'What about holding an exhibit?' " Aunt Bet prompted him.

"Yes, ma'am, I did. With a judge, and colored ribbons for first and second and third places. Maybe we could hold it before the vaudeville acts go on. Or maybe another time. We could tack up the pictures around the Playhouse."

"Why, Mac, what a wonderful idea!"

A lot of people liked the idea and said so.

"And I sort of thought," he went on, "why not ask someone like Mr. Purdy to be the judge? He knows photography, and he probably knows something about sketching, too. So all we'd need," Mac said with a disarming grin, "is a few yards of blue and red and yellow ribbon."

Cherry was the only camper who did not smile. Curious, she thought, that Mac Cook should avoid Purdy all along and now *suggest* that Purdy come to Blue Water. It didn't make sense.

She wished she knew more about Mac Cook. Who was he, really? What was he doing around here? Cherry urgently wanted to know.

With a lull at the infirmary, and a sweeping view of the camp and road, Cherry could watch what went on. Dr. Lowell had suggested that she take her paper work out on the porch. From there she saw a few unfamiliar cars drive into camp. This was the first week end parents were permitted to visit their children, and several parents were arriving for a long week end. They would stay at inns in nearby towns.

Since so many of the parents were expected, it had been decided to hold the picture exhibit this Saturday afternoon. Mr. Purdy had been invited to serve as judge. From the infirmary's porch Cherry saw girls from various cabins, and from the sketch group, carefully carry their pictures into the Playhouse. When Cherry looked in there at lunch hour, Mac was tacking them up on the walls. He seemed preoccupied and serious.

"The pictures look fine," Cherry said.

"Oh, it's you," Mac said, startled. "Yes, they do. The contest's from three to four today. They're going to serve lemonade afterward."

"Wish I could come," said Cherry, "but I'm on duty this afternoon. I'll watch from the hill."

He gave her a sharp look, took his hammer, and walked away without a word. Again, Cherry felt vaguely disturbed. She turned to the pictures. The pencil drawings of trees and hills were surprisingly good, and the snapshots made a vivid record of Blue Water life.

During the afternoon Cherry saw a short figure, shuffling along in rope sandals and crowned with a beret, walk into camp. It was Mr. Purdy. Cherry saw the photographer and the Wrights and some of the parents and children congregate around the Main House, then stroll over to the Playhouse. The exhibit was officially under way. A dozen other campers sacrificed their swim to attend.

The infirmary telephone rang. Jan Lowell answered, then said, "No, not up here. But I'll ask Cherry if she has." Jan came to the porch door. "Have you seen Mac Cook around?"

"Not since noon," Cherry said. "Why?"

"Bob Wright has had old Tom looking for Mac since two o'clock. Can't find him. Well, never mind." Jan went indoors again and Cherry returned to her records work with a divided mind.

So Mac was not at the Playhouse. Keeping out of Purdy's way? He'd ducked from Purdy once before. Cherry knew Mac was supposed to be at work this afternoon. He certainly was keeping himself well hidden. Or—it was possible—Mac might have slipped out of camp via some roundabout, out-of-sight path. Below her, Cherry saw all the camp vehicles parked around the Main House. That meant Mac had not driven anywhere on an errand. Where was he?

Mac did not turn up until suppertime, long after Purdy had left. Mac wore an innocent air, and his eyes widened when several people, leaving the Mess Hall, asked him where he'd been. Cherry was with them.

"Why, I was cleaning out the tool shed," Mac declared. "Go and see how good it looks now! Well, I can't help it if Tom didn't look for me there."

"Did look for you there," the old man grumbled. "Where in heck was you?"

Uncle Bob Wright was annoyed but he was a

mild-tempered man. "After this, Mac, leave word with Tom or with Sophie in the kitchen where you'll be. All right, go have your supper now."

"Thanks, I've had it. Do you need me any more this evening?" Mac asked. He was in a hurry to leave, for once. Cherry noticed that he hitched a ride in one of the parents' cars.

"My land," Sophie complained to Cherry, when

"Someone broke into my barn!"

she went to consult the cook about a special diet, "here I laid out Mac's supper and he didn't eat a bite of it! I declare I don't know what's got into that young fellow."

"Mac *was* in a hurry," Cherry murmured.

Half an hour later she thought she knew why.

Paul Purdy burst in at the camp entrance, out of breath and excited. He wanted to notify the

Everything is upside down!"

Wrights, he said, because maybe they knew who was responsible. He was so angry he sputtered.

"My barn—where I store my— Someone broke into my barn! Everything is upside down! Somebody ransacked the whole barn!"

Bob Wright came out on the steps of the Main House. Campers and counselors gathered round, curious.

"Why, Mr. Purdy, that's terrible! When did this happen?"

"This afternoon! While I was here judging the children's pictures!" Purdy shouted. "Did someone from here mess up my barn while I was away?"

Suddenly, Cherry saw, Purdy was no longer a jolly kewpielike little person but a man with a flash of savage temper.

Bob Wright said coldly, "I beg your pardon, Mr. Purdy, or perhaps you ought to beg mine. We have been neighbors for two summers, this is the third summer, and surely you know we are not people who break into barns."

"Yes, yes, yes. I am sorry, Mr. Wright. But you don't think it was any of the children who picked the lock, maybe to borrow costumes?"

"I seriously doubt that." Bob Wright's eyes flashed in his turn behind his glasses. "All of our campers are under constant supervision. Besides, they know they only need to *ask* you for costumes, since you are generous about lending them. I'll inquire, of course—but honestly, Mr. Purdy, you're overexcited."

"Well, maybe some of your employees—I think

it was a man, because the lock was broken. The heavy trunks in the barn were moved. What about the riding master?" Purdy went on. "What about the old handyman? That young man who teaches athletics?"

Cherry was struck by the fact that the photographer did not mention Mac Cook. It occurred to her that Purdy *did not know* Mac Cook was in the vicinity. So if Mac really were trying to dodge Purdy, he had succeeded.

The camp director was trying to soothe Paul Purdy. "If you'd like to use our telephone to notify the police—"

"No, no, no." Purdy brushed the suggestion aside. "Never mind the police just now. Thanks just the same. I guess—it's as you say—I am overexcited."

"But don't you want to report your losses?" Aunt Bet spoke up. "Was anything valuable taken?"

"I—I don't know." Purdy wiped his round, sweating face. "I searched the barn very quickly—hastily, you know, using my flashlight. In the morning I will look more carefully. Then I'll notify the state police."

"Yes, that's better," Bob Wright agreed. "We're awfully sorry about this, Mr. Purdy. Come on in and have some iced tea and catch your breath."

The photographer went into the Main House with the Wrights. The crowd drifted down to the water's edge, and forgot it.

But Cherry couldn't dismiss the incident so lightly. "Mac Cook wasn't anywhere to be found this afternoon," she thought. "I wonder if he did it? He was the one who suggested the picture exhibit in the first place. And it was he who thought we should get Mr. Purdy to be the judge. He gave a pretty lame excuse when he finally did show up. Uncle Bob is too easy with everybody."

For the first time, Cherry did not enjoy telling ghost stories around a bonfire. The rifling of Purdy's barn left her uneasy, even a little frightened. She recalled the sharp look Mac Cook had given her to-day when she had tried to talk to him about the exhibit, and she wondered what that look had meant.

CHAPTER VI

Faceless Clue

MAC COOK RETURNED TO WORK MONDAY MORN-
ing as if nothing had gone wrong. He was—or pro-
fessed to be—astounded at the rifling of Mr. Purdy's
storage barn. The hands at the Clemences' farm had
told him about it, Mac said, and so had the Eplers
whom he visited on Sunday. The whole neighborhood was buzzing with the news.

Naturally the three medical people discussed the
theft. Except that it was not exactly a theft, Dr.
Lowell reported. He had gone to see the camp director at midmorning, and Purdy had dropped by.

"Funny thing," said Dr. Lowell. "Purdy says nothing was taken, so far as he can determine. He says
the barn was ransacked, contents turned upside
down, but the thief didn't steal anything."

"How odd," Jan Lowell said. "What did the thief
break in for, then?"

"Maybe he was interrupted," Dr. Lowell said,

"and had to get out in a hurry before he could take anything."

"Or maybe it was a prank," Jan said.

Cherry kept her thoughts on the subject to herself.

"Well, whoever the thief was," Dr. Lowell said, "he didn't leave a clue in the barn."

"I don't like it," Cherry said to herself. "Even though Uncle Bob questioned Mac this morning, and seems entirely satisfied, I still don't like it."

And yet she had not clearly made up her mind about this young man. His rootless, evasive actions troubled her, but his kindness with the children half allayed her suspicions. It was Mac who, repairing the dock, went to rescue the Midgets' ducklings from the motorboat's propeller. It was Mac who could whistle the best of anyone, and knew how to fashion stick figures from gnarled roots and twigs.

Sue Howard liked him so well that she saved cookies from home to give him. "He's awfully nice to us, Miss Cherry," she said. "He repaired the spotlights at the Playhouse and put in rose, yellow, and blue slides for us. Just wait till you see the show! And when we told him about Katy's fern project— I mean we're going to plant ferns around our cabin— Mac told us where we'll find a whole hillside of ferns."

So the fern project was going to be acted upon. Cherry was interested. She was spending some time herself, these hot sunny afternoons, helping the girls collect natural-science specimens. Lake and woods provided an abundance of plant and animal life, more than the girls or even Jean Wheeler and Cherry could identify. When no one knew the name of the exquisite vine of white blossoms, up they went on the Can-You-Name-This Shelf in the Mess Hall where everyone could see. Everyone took a guess, and several campers were bright enough to consult the nature books in the camp library. The white blossoms turned out to be moonflower, slowly unfolding its petals at evening.

Evenings were particularly lovely along the lakeside, Cherry thought. The campers were in bed asleep, quiet settled over Camp Blue Water, and the lake shimmered with moonlight. Cherry had been promising herself for some time that she would go for a moonlight swim. On Wednesday evening, after a full day, she was longing for a dip.

The counselors who were not on duty were unwilling to come with her. "Too tired," Leona Jackson yawned. And Jean Wheeler said at their cabin window, "See those clouds in the west? We may have a thunder shower."

"I'll take a chance on it," Cherry said, and changed into her bathing suit.

She found it peaceful to swim alone in the deserted lake. Although a strong swimmer, she did not venture out to deep water when lake and beach were deserted. Cherry swam quietly, not splashing, so as not to disturb the occupants of the lake-front cabins. Sometimes she floated on her back, looking up at the stars, drifting in the cool water. Now and then a cloud floated over the face of the moon.

Or *was* the lake deserted? Wasn't that a rowboat

with a single figure pulling at the oars? Cherry spun around almost soundlessly in the water for a better look.

Yes, someone was out on the lake, late as it was. That was unusual. When the counselors rowed out in the evening, they went in groups. This was someone alone. Cherry strained to see who it was, but the distant figure—a man? a woman?—was indistinct as clouds darkened the view. She could see dim outlines—the rowboat looked ordinary enough, like any one of the camp boats or the boats which local people left tied up along the lake—

Just then, Cherry saw the rower make a throwing gesture, and a small splash sounded a moment afterward. Then the rowboat swung hard around and rapidly slid away. It vanished in the darkness.

Cherry was so astonished that she kept on treading water and watching, although she felt chilly and there was nothing left to see.

"The rower must have been a man," Cherry decided as she ran out of the water. "No woman could row as hard and fast as that."

She flung on her beach coat and gazed at the spot where she had seen the figure throw—throw what?—into deep water. She was tempted to swim out there, dive, and see what she could find. But that was something to do by daylight, when one could see to some degree underwater.

"I'll dive tomorrow," Cherry decided. She stood quite still for a moment, memorizing landmarks on this shore and on the opposite shore, in order to fix the spot where the stranger had halted the boat.

It was a shame to miss the vaudeville show next afternoon, yet in another way this hour gave her her best chance. The entire camp was pouring into the Playhouse, and the water front and lake were deserted. The day was brilliantly clear.

"Lucky thing I have the afternoon off," Cherry told herself as she again changed into her bathing suit. From her cabin she could hear visitors from Camp Thunder Cliff hiking in to see the girls' vaudeville show, and she also heard some station wagons arrive. Probably these were full of the smallest boys. She wondered if Reed Champion were driving. No matter. She had to make this hour count.

Cherry swam with long, easy strokes. Usually she swam with her hair free, but today she had her dark curls tucked tightly beneath a rubber cap, so no tendrils would obscure her vision. When she reached deep water, about midway across this long, relatively narrow lake, Cherry tread water and took her bearings. Yes, the landmarks tallied; this was just about the right place.

Now, how to allow for the thing's underwater drift? If she only had some inkling of its weight, its color, of what she must look for . . . She took a deep breath, jackknifed, and plunged down, keeping her eyes wide open. The water streaming past her grew greener as she forced her way toward the lake bed. The bottom proved to be sand; occasionally her hand touched large, smooth stones. It was hard to distinguish anything down here where water, sand, and stones all merged together in a dark blur. Cherry groped with her hands to seize a floating object—and rose to the surface to find she was holding a handful of grasses and roots.

She dove again. How far could the thing have drifted, she wondered as she swam slowly to and fro, holding her breath. What was that? Drifting just out of her reach? Only a waterlogged rag. She came up into the blinding sunshine for breath, then made a fresh attempt.

This time Cherry poked among the stones and she was lucky. She did find something caught, wedged, down there—something slippery and rather sickening to touch, but possessing a hard core. No telling what it was, except that it felt—not natural.

But when she came up to daylight, Cherry could not at first determine what it was she held. It was rubber and it was wrapped around something, tied by two strings. She untied the strings and saw that it was a flesh-colored oblong about as long as two hands together, with two holes in it near one edge. "What in the world," she thought. The object inside was only a stone, and she let that fall back into the water while she again examined her find.

Then it struck her. The thing was a mask. A faceless mask; simply a thin opaque sheath of rubber to be drawn over the face, with two eyeholes to see through.

"Cherry! What are you doing out there?"

Reed Champion stood on the shore, waving to her. Cherry tucked the mask in the neck of her swim suit and started toward him.

"Hi, Reed! Why aren't you at the show?"

"I did stay for part of it. Not the most professional performance anyone ever gave, but the kids enjoy home-grown talent." Reed gave her a hand as she came out of the water. "What *are* you doing out here by yourself?"

"Oh, just wanted a swim. I have the afternoon off."

"Want to drive to the village with me? I have to stop at the garage, and do a couple of errands. Come on. We could have a coke and a visit."

"Fine. I'll get dressed quickly."

She took the mask with her, in her purse.

Driving with Reed was pleasant—he handled the station wagon easily, slowing down considerably for bumps in the country road. In the village Reed left the station wagon for a quick checkup, and they strolled around the quiet leafy square.

"This sure is a peaceful town," Reed said. "Never a bit of excitement."

"A thief breaking into Mr. Purdy's barn caused quite a bit of excitement, don't you think? Reed, is there any chance that anyone from Thunder Cliff did it?" Cherry asked.

"Absolutely not." Reed seemed indignant. "We did discuss that with our fellows but—why, it's out of the question for several reasons. No, some outsider broke in."

But Reed was more interested in doing his errands, and presenting Cherry with a bottle of vivid strawberry pop than in discussing Mr. Purdy's troubles.

"If the color doesn't kill you, you'll find it's delicious," Reed said with a grin. "Me, I drink milk. That's for athletes who want to stay in training."

As they went around the shops, Cherry held on tightly to her purse, and turned over in her mind two or three possibilities about what to do with the mask. A plan began to take shape.

"You're awfully quiet," Reed said as they picked up the car at the garage.

"Why, most boys complain that girls talk too much," Cherry teased. "You're hard to please."

He smiled. Repartee was not for him. "You have something on your mind, I'd say."

"Yes, Reed, I have. Perhaps later on I'll ask your advice on it."

When they had driven almost within sight of Camp Blue Water, they saw Fred and Vernie Epler in a jeep bumping along toward them. The two cars stopped side by side.

"Hello, Cherry Ames!" Vernie called. "We haven't seen you lately. How are you?"

"Just fine, thanks. How are you and your pretty farm getting along?"

They chatted briefly about the crops and weather, about poor Mr. Purdy having his barn ransacked, about Mrs. Clemence's gladioli taking first prize at the church flower show.

"Has Mac Cook been around to see you lately?" Cherry asked, trying to be casual. She knew—or Mac had said—he had visited the Eplers last Sunday, but she was curious to know their reaction.

Vernie Epler seemed to hesitate, then said quickly, "Why, yes, Mac came over Sunday afternoon," and changed the subject. "I hear the vaudeville show was a great success."

"What! Is it over?" Reed exclaimed. "I'd better hurry up and pick up my boys. Excuse us, folks."

They said good-by and drove off in opposite directions. So Mac had told the truth about where he was on Sunday, if not on Saturday when the barn was rifled. Cherry wondered how the rubber mask fitted in with the raid on the barn—if it fitted in at all.

Just before supper that evening, Cherry put her plan into effect. She placed the mask on the Can-You-Name-This Shelf in the Mess Hall. To lessen the chance of its being stolen, she made a point of calling everyone's attention to the oddity.

"It looks like a homemade diving mask," Sue Howard speculated.

"Don't be silly," Mary Alice retorted. "It's just an old piece of bathing cap with holes in it."

Katy, who was clearly still playing Juliet in her mind's eye, stopped long enough to declare, "It's a theatrical property, that's what. An actor could paste a beard on it, or draw a clown face on it, or anything."

The person whom Cherry most wanted to see the mask—Mac Cook—did see it. He came in with a tray of desserts, helping Sophie, and paused in front of the shelf. He looked for a long time, not saying a word, his face noncommittal.

Cherry kept silent, too. She waited.

The next morning Mac came to see her at the infirmary.

"Miss Cherry, can you take a few minutes out to talk to me? Sort of privately?"

Dr. Lowell excused her. Cherry and Mac Cook strolled along a path which took them out of range of the campers. He seemed subdued and anxious.

"Yes, what is it, Mac?"

"The kids say you're the one who fished that mask out of the lake."

"Yes, I did. Do you think it *is* a mask?"

"Anyone can see it's a mask. Well, I wonder if you'd do me a favor. I wonder if you'd give me the mask? Please, Miss Cherry?"

"Whatever for?"

"It's not valuable. Anyone can make a mask like that. Once in New York I—" He caught himself. "I just want it for a joke, Miss Cherry."

"That doesn't seem like much of a reason."

He faced her almost despairingly. "What kind of reason do I have to give you? Honestly, I want it for just an innocent—joke."

"See here, Mac Cook. Did you throw that mask in the lake?"

Her question came so unexpectedly that he was stunned. His eyes blazed. "No, I didn't! But I can tell you who did! It was Purdy."

"Purdy? Do you expect me to believe that? What makes you think it was Purdy?" Cherry demanded.

"For a very good reason. I know it was Pep. Only I can't tell you how I know."

Cherry saw that Mac Cook was nearly in tears. The mask must be terribly important to him.

"I know what you're thinking," Mac said angrily. "You think I'm the one who broke into the barn, and you think I used the mask to cover up while I did the job. Well, it's not so! The mask has nothing at all to do with the barn. It isn't even my mask! It belongs to Purdy. I swear it, Miss Cherry."

His voice held the ring of truth, but perhaps he was only a clever actor. Cherry sighed, and sat down on a log.

"If it's Purdy's mask, why should I give it to you? No, Mac, I'm sorry, but unless you can give me some believable explanation for all this—"

"What do you care? That's my business."

"It might also be my business if I should get our neighbor, Mr. Purdy, into trouble. I must say, Mac, you've behaved strangely—ducking when Purdy came into sight at the greenhouse that time—staying out of the way when he came to judge the picture exhibit—"

"If you knew the truth, Miss Cherry, you wouldn't blame me for ducking."

Mac sat down beside her and put his head in his hands. This young man was in trouble. Cherry felt a surge of unreasonable sympathy for him; she steeled herself against it. Mac's entire behavior was suspicious, the stories he told were vague and wild.

"Listen, Miss Cherry. I realize the way I'm acting doesn't make any sense to you," he said, with that extraordinary sensitivity—or cleverness?—of his. "But honestly there's a reason—if I could tell you."

It seemed to Cherry that if the reason were an honest or valid one, Mac would not need to keep it secret. Blameless people did not go skulking around as Mac Cook was doing. But Cherry kept still and let him talk.

"Miss Cherry, do you know if Paul Purdy came here directly from New York?"

"I don't know. Even if I did know," she said stiffly, "I'm not sure I should tell you. I *can* tell you that Mr. Purdy is known and respected around here."

"Yes, sure he is," Mac agreed. He plucked at a piece of twine, brooding. "Will you change your mind and let me have the mask? Please!"

"I'm sorry, Mac, but I can't do that."

Cherry walked away, leaving him sitting there. He seemed discouraged rather than angry.

She did not think Mac would harm her in an effort to possess the mask. Did he, though, intend some harm to Paul Purdy? Secrecy would be essential. Why all the protests of innocence? To mislead her and keep her from talking? Or was there a chance that Mac was innocent—that the mask did belong to Purdy? That certainly appeared unlikely.

Cherry at once removed the mask from the Can-You-Name-This Shelf. She put it in an envelope, sealed the envelope, and asked Uncle Bob to keep it for her in the safe. That mask might come in handy one of these days, she thought, remembering the newspaper article she had read. No mention of a mask was made, but the two women employees had said that the thief had appeared featureless.

Could a mask like this make one appear featureless? Cherry believed it could.

~~~~~~

CHAPTER VII

Look Out for Trouble

THE GRAY KITTEN WAS EXPLORING CAUTIOUSLY, DEL-icately, among the cool ferns at dusk, outside of the Mountaineers' cabin. When Cherry saw the silky little creature jump at a fern frond, pretending to be a tiger, she looked more closely at the ferns.

"So Katy completed her project," Cherry said to herself. "Good for her!"

There were repercussions.

The first thing Cherry knew early the next morning was Sue Howard saying in an aggrieved voice outside her window:

"*Was* it your idea, Miss Cherry? Hey! Are you awake?"

"I'm awake, all right, especially with you talking in my ear," Cherry said. "Whatever is the matter?"

"Oh. Sorry. But *did* you give Katy those ideas? I mean, it was very nice of her to suggest land-scaping our cabin. And Mary Alice *does* appreciate

Katy's straightening her bunk shelf for her, even
if Katy did accidentally spill Mary Alice's bottle of
toilet water. But *are you responsible* about the ferns?"

"Ferns were Katy's idea, and I admit I encouraged
her."

At first the Mountaineers praised Katy's efforts,
Sue said, and welcomed her awkward efforts to be
friends. "We said if Katy'd try, we'd try."

Searching for the ferns in the woods had been
fun. But digging them up had led to an argument.
Katy wanted to supervise the job; the other girls
felt she was not doing her share of the work. Lil
arbitrated. But when lugging the filled bushel baskets back to camp had produced blisters on their
hands, Katy had complained loudest of all.

"Oh, that Katy! She was bearable last week, as
long as she thought she was Juliet. But now she's
her old cranky self again," Sue sighed.

"If you go on disliking her," Cherry said, "all
you'll ever have is warfare. Do you want that?" Sue
shook her head. "Believe it or not, Sue, I have an
idea a sensitive, friendly girl is buried somewhere
inside Katy."

"Buried awfully deep," Sue observed, in a discouraged voice.

"Yes, but trying to come out. I know you've tried
to be patient and helpful, but were *you* the perfect
camper, your first season at Blue Water?"

"N-no. I guess," Sue said quickly, "for Katy it's
harder than for others. That's what Lil Baker told
us. All right, Cherry, we Mountaineers will do our
best for Katy, even if it kills us. She *is* doing better."

As Cherry predicted, Katy was trying hard to be less selfish. Sue and Ding treated her with a new respect, and Mary Alice forgave the wasted toilet water. But Katy had her lapses. The girls never could be sure what to expect from her. If it had not been for Mac Cook, snatching a blanket roll out of the fire at the woodcraft area, Katy would have paid dearly for her carelessness. They were using the blanket roll to practice how to handle it and how to choose the best spot for sleeping outdoors, for their forthcoming overnight hike.

"You really ought to be a little more careful," Sue told Katy worriedly. "You *know* we have to pass our skills tests, to go along on the hike."

"I'm going on that hike." Katy tossed her head a little. "I'll be just as skillful as anybody else. Notice that I know how to make a fire that *lasts*."

Sue bit her lip to keep from making an unkind answer; Jean Wheeler and Cherry intervened. Cherry had been giving them a little talk, warning about poison ivy, and poisonous berries and mushrooms, and in general how to take care of one's health in the open. Jean Wheeler, the hiking master, went on to describe the shelters they would use on the trail.

"The boys from Thunder Cliff built them, other summers, and they did a good job. If it rains or turns cold, we could live comfortably in those shelters for as long as we had to."

As the Intermediates practiced, Mac reinforced a stone fireplace at the end of the woodcraft area. Cherry sensed Mac Cook listening and watching.

Ever since the conversation about the mask, Mac Cook had been half avoiding her. That mask weighed on Cherry's conscience. She had been turning over in her mind the question of discussing it with the camp director. She had even been thinking of mentioning it—guardedly—to Mr. Purdy. But she saw no use in stirring up trouble over, quite possibly, nothing. If the mask had carried any identifying marks, that would be another matter. But the mask alone was a blind article. It was Mac Cook's actions which—again!—were revealing.

Cherry was walking along the road late one evening with Leona Jackson and Jean Wheeler, having a stroll before turning in. All this first week of August had been hot, even at this elevation. The cool, dark evening was a relief. Lights were out in the neighborhood farmhouses; the stretch of greenery which lay between the road and the water was deserted. In this peaceful place the three young women were startled by the wail of a siren.

"What's that?" Jean Wheeler trained her flashlight down the road toward the noise. "Police? Fire engine?"

"Step back into the grass!" Leona Jackson pulled at Cherry's arm.

They quickly got off the road as the wailing vehicle rushed toward them. It flashed past and turned sharply into the hills, screaming as it went.

"The state police," Jean Wheeler said. "It looks as if they're heading for that disreputable tavern where a fight broke out last summer."

She swung her flashlight in a wide arc around

the road. Out of the dark a man came running across the flashlight's beam—a yellow-haired man running in panic—running away from the lake front.

"Why, it's Mac Cook!" exclaimed Leona.

"I thought he went home to the Clemences' hours ago," Jean Wheeler said. "And what's he running like a scared rabbit for? Hi, Mac!"

But he did not stop running nor look back. The flashlight's beam could not extend far enough to follow him. Mac Cook vanished in the shadows.

"He's a crazy kid," Leona remarked. "Come on. Let's go home. It's late and we have quite a piece to walk."

"Mac was probably coming back from a late swim," Jean Wheeler said, "and the police siren startled him. Startled me, too." She chuckled.

But why, Cherry thought, *did a police siren frighten Mac Cook so much that he fled in panic?*

What had he been doing at the lake's edge? Not swimming, for she had seen that his hair was dry. Cherry would have liked to go and look around the water's edge where Mac had appeared from, but her companions were starting back to camp. She tried to remember whether he had been carrying anything— perhaps a fishing rod—but she wasn't sure.

Thursday afternoon was free time for Cherry. She hitched a ride with Vernie Epler, whom she met on the road, and drove with Vernie toward the village.

"Did you hear that siren last night?" Cherry asked.

"Wasn't it enough to wake the dead!" Vernie agreed. "Those shiftless people at the tavern, again.

Mrs. Brenner, who lives a mile from there, called me up and told me the police padlocked that awful place. Thank goodness."

"I thought possibly someone had broken into Mr. Purdy's barn again," Cherry said, and waited for Vernie's reply.

"Not that I know of," Vernie Epler said. She did not speak again until she headed the jeep into the village. She asked Cherry where she could let her off.

"The drugstore, if that's convenient for you." The jeep stopped and Cherry jumped out. "Thanks a lot. It was fun to see you." *Even though we had very little conversation*, Cherry thought.

"Nice to see *you*," Vernie said politely. She drove off, down the village street.

"Now I have no reason to suspect Vernie Epler of anything," Cherry scolded herself. "Vernie simply didn't feel like chatting, that's all. Why, the Eplers are among the most solid citizens around here."

She concluded that Mac Cook's actions were making her so suspicious that she'd be wary of the birds and butterflies next, if she didn't watch out!

As though she had conjured him up just by thinking of him, Mac Cook stood in the drugstore, with his back to her, busily making a purchase. It gave Cherry a turn to see him so unexpectedly. Though wasn't it always at unusual times and places that Mac appeared, with some weak excuse?

Why was Mac Cook in the village during his working hours? Had the Wrights sent him in on an errand? At the moment Mac was buying, of all things, a bottle of hair bleach. There were no synthetic blonds in camp. Was Mac Cook buying the hair bleach for himself?

Cherry looked carefully at his hair. Why, of course, it was dyed! It showed dark at the scalp—she had never noticed this before. And the mustache, too, must belatedly need a touch-up.

She felt her heart pounding with excitement or with fear. The false blondness now pointed toward an open attempt at deception. All along she had felt doubtful about the young man's doings but had been unable to prove anything. Now, today, here at a prosaic drugstore counter, she had stumbled onto the fact that he was trying to conceal his identity.

"Hello, Mac," she said, trying to sound as usual.

"Great balls of fire! You again!" He faced her, trying to smile. "We seem to meet all the time. Well—" Mac Cook was flustered. "I—ah—I'm in the village because I have to buy supplies for one of the kids' birthday party. This Saturday."

Cherry nodded and said, laughing, "You certainly use colorful language. What was that expression— 'Great balls of fire'?"

But Cherry did not really feel like laughing, for she remembered all too clearly that *the loan company robber, when confronted by the two women, had pulled a gun and said, "Great balls of fire! Get in that door and keep still!"*

"I didn't use any expression like that." Mac Cook had turned pale as a ghost. "You heard me wrong, Miss Cherry."

"Perhaps I did," Cherry said pleasantly.

The drugstore clerk came to give Mac the wrapped package and his change. Mac seemed relieved at the interruption. He held up the package jokingly.

"Tooth powder, but not for the birthday party."

Cherry knew it wasn't tooth powder, but she said nothing.

They walked together to the door. "Didn't you come in here to buy something?" Mac asked.

"Yes. I'm in no hurry," Cherry said.

"Or did you come in here to spy on me?" His voice was low, so only Cherry could hear, and trembling with anger. "If you knew the whole story, you wouldn't—"

"Then why don't you tell me the whole story?" Cherry had to control her own temper. "See here, Mac, I'm not spying on you. But what do you expect me to think when you ask me for the mask I fished out of the lake, and now when I find you buying hair dye, not tooth powder? What would *you* think?"

"The worst." He held the door open for her. They went outdoors together as if nothing were happening. "I can tell you this much. If you go to Purdy and tell him what you know about me—well—"

"Well, what?"

"You'll be making an awful mistake. Don't do it. There's too much at stake. Don't tip off Purdy!"

"I don't like being threatened, Mac Cook!" Cherry burst out. He tried to protest but she would not be stopped. "I know you're afraid of something. Anybody would know after seeing you run down the road the other night when the state police car—"

"So it was *you!* Who else saw?" Mac demanded.

"Two other counselors." Poor Mac. He was still a ghastly color, and his eyes pleaded like the eyes of an injured animal. Guilty or innocent, she pitied him. "Take it easy, Mac. The other two girls didn't give it a second thought."

"But you did. Are you going to report me?"

"I don't know yet," Cherry said. "I have to think."

Mac went on talking with an effort. Cherry let him change the subject.

"Sue Howard's going to have a birthday party," he said. "Surprise party, I guess. But she's sharp, she'll probably guess it. Well, I have to get along to the grocery store. Sophie wants some extra supplies."

Mac and Cherry parted, Cherry deep in thought. Where did her duty lie? Should she report her suspicions to Uncle Bob? If she did, he probably would fire Mac and perhaps call in the police. And this, if Mac were innocent of any real wrongdoing, could do him great harm. But dared she wait, thus exposing the campers to possible harm and becoming in effect an accessory to what might have been Mac's crime?

So preoccupied was Cherry that she completely forgot to make her purchases and walked all the way back to camp, mulling over her problem as she went along.

Finally, she came to a decision. "I believe," she said to herself, "that I will wait a little longer. I'll watch Mac as much as I can, and try to get some real evidence. All I have now are suspicions, and I'd hate to jeopardize a man's reputation on suspicions alone."

With her mind made up, Cherry entered the infirmary, determined to find out the real truth about Mac Cook.

So much noise, so many voices floated out of the Mountaineers' cabin even after Lights Out that Cherry guessed Sue knew all about the "surprise" party. The clamor sounded too cheerful for squabbling with Katy. Friday night's efforts at sleep were punctuated by that cabin's bursts of song:

> "Goodness me, why what was that?
> Silent be, it was the cat!
> It was, it *was* the cat!
> They're right, it *was* the *ca-a-at!!*"

Then Lil Baker's exasperated voice: "This is no time to sing *Pinafore*." There was a brief silence, followed by smothered giggles which Cherry could hear clear across the path in her own cabin. Well, with all these high spirits, and even allowing for tiffs with Katy, Sue's birthday party promised to be a merry occasion.

The entire camp was invited. Some brother campers of the same age were asked, too, including D. V. who, in tribute to Sue, brought the saxophone that he played in his school band. It was a perfect summer's afternoon. Sophie had just finished icing several birthday cakes, and Mac carried them to public view on the Mess Hall tables.

"Can't put these gorgeous cakes on the Can-You-Name-This Shelf, can we?" Mac said. He was enjoying the fun as much as anybody.

D. V.'s saxophone solo was not very professional, nor was Katy's rendition of *Juliet*, but at least they added to the merriment. The Intermediates and Juniors played a far-flung game of hide-and-seek, fanning out over hill and meadow. Then they played baseball, while the Seniors looked on with dignity and the younger campers had their naps. Sue, the guest of honor, admitted she felt thrilled at attaining the age of twelve.

"Now it's only a year to wait until I enter my teens," Sue said. Mountaineer or not, she had tied a ribbon in her hair today.

There was still an hour to go before suppertime when the campers sat down in the grass to hold a sing.

Just before suppertime, Mr. Purdy trotted into camp with his small camera slung around his neck. Aunt Bet escorted him to the big singing circle.

"Yes, there's still plenty of light to take pictures," Cherry heard Paul Purdy say. He waved at the children, who called hello's to the oddly garbed little man.

Pep looked like an amiable pixie in his beret and thick-soled sandals. The lines in his face, Cherry noticed, spelled something else again. Was Purdy older than one would suppose? Ill? Worried about something? But he seemed in good spirits as he threaded his way toward Sue and her cronies.

"Take me and my kitten!" Katy stepped forward.

"I'll get the kitten—excuse me, Sue. I mean, *after* you take the birthday pictures, Mr. Purdy."

No one paid much attention to Katy. D. V. and some of the other boys crowded around, asking how the precision camera worked. Aunt Bet hoped aloud that some of today's pictures could be used for the camp catalogue.

"Mac!" Aunt Bet called, and waved to Mac in the Mess Hall. "Will you bring a birthday cake, please? Nice touch for the pictures, Mr. Purdy."

Several minutes passed. Mac did not come out with a birthday cake.

"Where is he? Oh, bother," said Aunt Bet. "Will someone go over and bring a cake?"

"I'll go," said Cherry, before anyone else could.

She ran. She was not a moment too soon. Bursting into the kitchen, she found Mac gathering up his jacket and work shoes, and Sophie railing at him.

"You can't quit now, Mac! We have to give the kids their supper! Can't you wait half an hour? What's got into you?"

"I can't wait," Mac muttered. Then he saw Cherry.

"I came for a cake," she said.

"You'll— cake—? Thanks. Gee, thanks a lot."

"What's going on here?" Sophie demanded.

"I'd like to know, too, Mac," said Cherry.

He set down his things for an instant. "I— It's like this, Miss Cherry. I don't want you to think badly of me. I just got word, just today, to hurry back to the city. To New York. At lunch hour I asked Fred Epler to take me to the train. It just dawned on me that if I don't hurry, I'll miss my train. That's how it is. You see, Miss Cherry?"

"But what about collecting your pay?" Sophie asked. "Aren't you going to say good-by to the Wrights? And the kids? Running out on us—"

Mac and Cherry continued to look at each other, measuring each other.

"Here comes Aunt Bet," said Sophie with satisfaction. "With Mr. Purdy and Sue's crowd. I'll bet they're going to take pictures at their table. Flashbulb pictures, I'll bet."

Aunt Bet called, "Sophie! Mac! Come in and be in the picture, too!"

Mac bolted out the back door. He was already halfway to the road when Aunt Bet and Purdy walked in, looking for him.

"Mac Cook is running away," Sophie blurted out to Aunt Bet. "Look! There he goes!"

Cherry was watching Paul Purdy. He did not react at all to the name of Mac Cook, to her surprise. When he joined Aunt Bet to watch the running man with the thatch of yellow hair, Purdy still did not react.

"Let him go," Aunt Bet said with a sigh. "Transient help—most of them leave without notice. It's happened to us so many times."

"But why is he running?" Purdy asked. He was genuinely puzzled.

Cherry asked Aunt Bet in a low voice, "Did Mac do anything—out of order?"

"No, he was a good worker, in fact quite wonderful with the children."

By now Mac had disappeared from sight. He had, Cherry noted, headed in the direction of the Eplers' house. Perhaps there was a degree of truth in his story about hurrying to catch a train.

An emergency—*what emergency?* Wasn't the narrow squeak of meeting Purdy the real emergency? Cherry suspected that it was.

About one thing Cherry was especially curious. Purdy had not recognized Mac by name or by appearance, at least not at a distance. Was that because Purdy had never met Mac? Or was it because Mac had dyed his hair and assumed another name?

How very strange, if Purdy did not know there existed a man who was so urgently and nervously interested in him! Was that possible?

It occurred to Cherry that she knew almost nothing about Purdy. Perhaps if she could learn a few facts about Purdy, they might very well shed light on the mystery of Mac Cook.

"Except that I could hardly go spying on the camp's good neighbor," Cherry thought uncomfortably.

~~~~~~

CHAPTER VIII

A Lesson for Katy

IT WAS ALMOST MORE THAN THE MOUNTAINEERS could bear. After all the practice time spent learning woodcrafts and campfire cooking, it rained without letup on Sunday, Monday, and Tuesday! Besides that, Katy and Mary Alice had not yet passed their tests. Until they did, no overnight hike for them.

"Every week I've watched hikers set forth," Mary Alice wailed, "and now when it's *our* turn, I can't —we can't—go!"

Their cabin loyally decided to wait a few days longer until Mary Alice and Katy caught up with the others' skills. Jean Wheeler pointed out in her calm way that she would not lead them into half-wild country in a drenching rainstorm, anyway.

Cherry felt as impatient as the Mountaineers, for this was the trip on which she was invited to go along. Dr. Lowell and Bob Wright had given her clearance from her job, charged against her time off.

The rest of the campers were restless, too. Girls took turns making cookies until Sophie declared, "We have enough brownies on hand for next summer, too." Many of the girls were worried about their gardens at the Model Farm in this downpour; their prize tomatoes and corn must be just ripe for picking. Mrs. Clemence telephoned to say their handyman was harvesting this crop for Blue Water, but that meant losing half the fun. In the crafts shops, during this rainy stretch, the campers produced a record for scratched, bruised, scorched, and scraped fingers. As Cherry cleansed and treated these, she wondered whether the injuries were not caused mostly by exasperation with the rain.

The delay did give her a chance to observe some interesting things related—directly? indirectly?—to Mac Cook.

Mac had disappeared on Saturday, August tenth, just before suppertime. Just after supper Cherry had been strolling along the road with two bunk mates and had seen Fred Epler in his jeep. She wondered how Fred could have driven Mac all the way to the railroad station and be back home in so short a time. Cherry had waved, but Fred Epler had merely waved back, and driven on. He hadn't been so reticent earlier in the summer, it seemed to Cherry.

Then, that night, Thunder Cliff counselors had brought their boys over for the square dance. Cherry was on duty that evening in the infirmary. Reed Champion came running up the hill to say hello.

"Sorry you can't come down and dance," Reed had said.

"I offered to stay here. Bob and Jan Lowell love to dance."

"Well, then, I think I'll stick around and chat. What's new at Blue Water?"

"The interesting news—at least I think it's interesting—is that Mac Cook quit his job today, without any warning at all."

Cherry told Reed what had happened. He listened, rubbing his chin.

"That's funny," he said. "One of our campers was called home and I took the boy to the train. About five forty-five, same train as Mac must've wanted to catch. Matter of fact, it's the *only* daily train to New York. But I didn't see Mac at the station," Reed said. "No, I'm certain I didn't. I saw two elderly women board the train, and that's all."

"Maybe Mac missed the train," Cherry suggested. "Did you see Fred Epler's jeep at the station?"

"No, I didn't. Didn't see the jeep on the road, either—either going or coming. I would have, you know—we all use the same highway. But what do you find so interesting about Mac Cook? He's just a nice average guy. Maybe slightly peculiar, but what of it?"

Cherry made a sudden decision. "Reed," she said, "I'm not sure he is just a 'nice average guy.' I can't keep this bottled up any longer. I've got to tell someone. Listen—"

Cherry told him what she knew and what she suspected about Mac Cook. When she finished, Reed shook his head.

"It's too deep for me. But if there's anything I

can do to help Bob—or you—in case this Cook fellow makes any trouble for you—"

"Not so far." Cherry had checked and found the rubber mask still in its sealed envelope in the camp safe.

"I just don't know what to think." Reed glanced at his wrist watch and stood up hurriedly to leave. "Gosh, Cherry, I'm late. Excuse me? And don't forget, I'm around if you need me."

"Thanks a lot, Reed. I'm glad to know that."

A third fragment of information turned up on Tuesday, when Cherry, plagued by questions of Mac Cook's relationship to Purdy, visited Purdy himself. She dropped by the photographer's place at lunch hour, when the rain had temporarily ceased.

It was easy to find Mr. Purdy because there in the mud, fresh footprints of his rope-soled sandals led to his storage barn. Cherry heard sounds of hammering. He was standing outside the door of the barn.

"Hello, Mr. Purdy! Have you a minute to spare for a Blue Water caller?"

Paul Purdy turned around, hammer in hand.

"Hello, Miss Nurse. I am just putting a stronger lock on my barn door, as you see." Apparently he was still upset about the breaking-in incident. If he was annoyed at Cherry's interruption, it showed only in his being more abrupt than usual. "What can I do for you?"

"Perhaps you would advise me about the best way to use my camera," she said, holding it out.

It was an innocent ruse, and it did gain the photographer's interest. After a few minutes' talk about camera techniques, Purdy was in a better temper. Cherry thanked him, and ventured onto a less safe subject.

"That looks like a good, strong lock you're installing, Mr. Purdy."

"It had better be. It cost me enough. I've put on two other locks, ever since my barn was turned upside down. But they did not satisfy me. This lock is the best one made."

Cherry was puzzled. Three locks in the few weeks since the thief had broken in—and taken nothing, according to Mr. Purdy. Three locks, yet he had not bothered to call the police! Also, so far as Cherry could determine, Purdy still did not know that Mac Cook had been living in the vicinity. Or if Purdy knew about Mac Cook, was he indifferent? Cherry could not understand how this funny little man reasoned.

Purdy did not look quite so funny and jolly as he resumed work on the new lock. He struck hammer blows with grim purpose. On the ground, Cherry noticed, was a box containing other locks, of a type suitable for the barn windows.

"I've never been inside your fabulous barn, Mr. Purdy. The children seem to think it's a treasure house."

"You are welcome to look in," Purdy said, hammering away. "Just costumes and properties, and old negatives. They are not very valuable—not even valuable enough to insure—except to me. To me, they are my livelihood, you understand. It took me years to accumulate them, and just now—"

"Yes?" Cherry encouraged.

"Well, just now I cannot afford to buy new props," Purdy said.

That registered with Cherry. She had assumed, as did the other neighbors, that Purdy must be fairly prosperous since he owned this summer place and took a long vacation from his business. But he had just said that he was not well off "just now." Still—

"I imagine the cost of replacing the whole barn full of props would run into a large sum," Cherry said. "If I may—?"

She stepped into the dim barn. It was not a large place, but it was filled to overflowing with all sorts of curiosities: a suit of armor, a tambourine, dusty theatrical costumes, a dummy window and curtains, a flight of six carpeted steps, bunches of artificial flowers, painted backdrops, odd chairs. Mr. Purdy called to Cherry that from time to time he had had many actors and dancers and singers among his clientele, hence the theatrical props.

"I can't keep all this stuff in my studio. I bring it here, a few pieces at a time, in a friend's station wagon."

"Well, thanks for letting me have a look," said Cherry. "Now I know why the children are so fascinated."

Yet she had noted nothing in the barn which could explain why Mac Cook showed such a curious, evasive interest in Purdy.

On Wednesday a hot sun shone. Leaves ceased to drip, the earth dried out. On Wednesday, furthermore, Katy and Mary Alice passed their skills tests. Now, said Jean Wheeler, finally and at last, the Mountaineers cabin could pack to start the next day on their overnight hike.

"I can't believe it," said Sue to Cherry. "We're all so happy! Get ready, Cherry."

"I will. I'm not taking much along."

While Cherry got out her sturdiest shoes and borrowed a mess kit Wednesday evening, she received running reports from the cabin across the path. The kitten, in their absence, would be cared for by the Dingdong Belles. Lil Baker was *not* going along; Jean Wheeler and Cherry would accompany the six girls. Sophie was setting aside food for them to pack at the last minute: eggs, butter, pancake mix, bacon, cocoa, salt and pepper, flour, corn, and potatoes.

And Katy Osborn caused an uproar in her cabin by packing into her duffle bag extra shoes and a collapsible hammock—then found she could scarcely lift the duffle bag to her shoulder, much less walk with it. Cherry heard Katy snap:

"Aren't I trying?"

"Yes, very!" Sue snapped back.

Cherry thought of an old camp saying: "You never know a person until you have camped with her."

The next morning the weather was glorious and all six girls were in an angelic temper. After breakfast they lined up, packs on their backs, cooking equipment and blankets divided among them, their hatbrims pulled down against the sun. Cherry carried in her pack the first-aid kit and a small hatchet in a leather case. Jean Wheeler, with whistle and compass in her hand, took her place at the head of the line. The girls started off, the pride and envy of the camp, heading for mountain trails.

The sun rose higher as they marched along, singing and joking. Having left the main road a half mile outside of Blue Water, and crossed Long Lake at its narrowest point by an old footbridge, they found themselves climbing in unexpectedly wild country. This land, Jean Wheeler explained, was too steep to farm and too rocky for grazing.

It was beautiful here. Wild flowers grew among the rock ledges. At this height, the sky seemed bluer than usual. Cloud shadows floated across the band of girls who sometimes scrambled upward, sometimes followed a line of trees down to a shady brook. Sounds of a waterfall reached them.

"I'm thirsty," Katy said.

"You're suggestible," Jean Wheeler said. "Only small sips of water out of your canteens, girls."

On a rocky plateau with a magnificent view, they stopped for lunch. The sandwiches tasted wonderful. Then Jean led them down to a stream where they splashed cool water on their faces and hands. Since this water had not been analyzed on earlier hikes, they did not drink any of it.

During the afternoon, trails led them to sheer drops which took their breath away—through green glens and wild thickets. They were heading in the general direction of a shelter area, but exploring a new route to reach it. Jean Wheeler marked trees with the hatchet along the way.

"That's so we'll find our trail back, tomorrow."

"Back!" said Mary Alice. "We aren't even there yet. It's funny how much heavier my pack has gotten."

Their pace grew slower, stops more frequent. Jean Wheeler encouraged them by pointing out a tiny log shack nestled in a fold of the hills.

They reached this place at about four o'clock. The shelter turned out to be three-walled, not so tiny, a little lopsided. The Thunder Cliff boys who had built it had carved their initials and camp name on a center plank. Remains of earlier fires were evident. All the girls, even Katy and Mary Alice, who were the tiredest of the party, set down their packs and explored the camping area. Cherry and Jean Wheeler unpacked gear for supper.

No one except Cherry bothered to investigate the shelter. It was there just in case of rain or cold; unfurnished, it offered only a fireplace area of stones and a few empty shelves. Empty? Cherry caught sight of something red and went to look on the shelf. She found a three-day-old local newspaper and a large red calico handkerchief, the kind farmers buy in general stores. It was freshly washed but unironed. For no particular reason, Cherry shoved the handkerchief into her slacks pocket.

"Everybody come with me to the spring for a drink of water!" Jean called.

After a drink, they returned to the shelter area, took off their shoes and socks, and had a good rest in the grass. The only girl with a blister beginning on her heel was Cherry herself. She applied antiseptic ointment and a Band-aid, and fell asleep.

When they awoke—or rather, when Katy wakened them—the sun was rapidly sinking behind a mountain peak.

"It's a good thing Katy woke us," Jean Wheeler said. "We have a great deal to do before we can get our supper—and it's not a good idea to go stumbling through the woods by flashlight."

The group split up into teams. Their practice at Blue Water came in handy. Dee and Dot Smith, the twins, took buckets from inside the shelter and went to haul water for cooking and washing. Katy and Ding chose a site—a natural clearing on dry ground—and when Jean Wheeler approved, started digging with their heels a V-shaped slot for building a fire. Mary Alice hunted for flat stones to place there to hold in the heat. Meanwhile, Cherry and Sue had started into the forest to collect firewood.

Shadows already lay among the twisted aisles of tree trunks. At the edge of the forest Cherry and Sue saw only green wood, which burns poorly; they pushed deeper into the woods in search of dead twigs and bark for kindling, and dry branches for a cooking fire. The hush was profound.

"It's scary in here," Sue said to Cherry. Her voice sounded loud and thin.

"Nothing to be scared of," Cherry answered. "But let's be quick and not linger."

They picked up wood quickly, without talking. Sue wandered off to one side. Cherry could not see her for a few minutes. Then she heard a sharp crackle and splintering, as if someone had tripped.

"Sue! Did you fall?"

"No. I thought *you* fell."

Cherry stood motionless. Sue, coming toward her, saw and stood still, too. Somewhere ahead of them, the underbrush stirred and snapped again.

"An animal?" Sue whispered.

"Look!"

A man was running—running away from them —awkwardly in the dense growth of the forest. The fading light made it impossible for them to see anything but a blurred figure with a hat pulled down low. Was he carrying something or not? The man slipped out of sight behind the sweeping branches of fir trees.

Cherry breathed a sigh of relief. At least he was not eager to meet them, any more than she and Sue wished to meet him.

"Probably a tramp," Cherry said to Sue. "Better than a bear! Come on, though. We're not going to stay here and ask for trouble."

Cherry reported the incident to Jean Wheeler and also mentioned finding the handkerchief and old newspaper in the shelter. It seemed likely that the man had made himself at home in their shelter.

Jean was a little annoyed, but calm and unworried. "We ought to put up a *No Trespassing* sign, but he probably won't cause any trouble since he ran away from you."

Cheered by the savory smell of supper, Cherry stopped thinking about the figure in the forest.

A more immediate crisis was that Katy had forgotten to bring a cup or a dish to eat from.

"Well, Katy," said her partner, Mary Alice, "you straightened up my shelf in the cabin. Here, we'll take turns with my things."

Katy accepted the offer, though her pride was hurt. But she tried to be particularly helpful, watching that Mary Alice's and Sue's biscuits did not burn (they had wrapped dough in a spiral around a long twig), then digging the baked potatoes and ears of corn out of the ashes for the others. It was obvious to everyone that Katy was making a real effort to do her share.

Spiced with the fresh mountain air and pungent wood smoke, the food tasted better than anything served at the Mess Hall, and the girls ate ravenously as they sat around the fire in the gathering darkness.

"I'll help the cleanup squad," Katy volunteered, when they had finished.

Cherry went to help Katy scrub the pans. She found the erstwhile Juliet crying, under cover of darkness.

"Now, now," Cherry softly comforted her. "You're doing fine."

"Th-thanks. I'm crying because everybody is so nice to me. I don't deserve it."

"Yes, you do. And you'll come to deserve it still more."

"I—I—thought I didn't need anybody. But out here in the forest you'd starve or get lost without friends."

"But look what you're doing for them. They need you, too," Cherry said softly.

Out of the silence came Katy's surprised voice.

A man was running away from them

"I guess they do, a little bit, don't they? Lately when I tried to do things for them, I thought it was sort of to *buy* their friendship but—but—it's better than that."

"Much better," Cherry agreed. "You count, too, Katy."

"You mean I count not only as Katy, but as one of the Mountaineers—that's it!"

"Right! Now I wonder if we can make this old skillet shine?"

The stars came out. The girls sat cross-legged around the fire and toasted marshmallows on green twigs, and talked in the firelight.

"How far do you think we've come today?" Jean Wheeler asked them. "Can any of you sketch a map of the route we've taken?"

Sue did fairly well, sketching lines in the dirt. Jean Wheeler made a few corrections. They had hiked only a few miles; actually they were still quite close to Blue Water.

"We stopped too often," the Smith twins said solemnly.

The crude observation map set Cherry to thinking. That man she'd seen running away in the woods —he, too, was quite near to Blue Water and also to Purdy's barn. If someone wanted to rifle that barn, or attempt other thefts, what more logical way than to hide nearby at this lonely outpost and await his chance? Or perhaps the man was simply, as she'd said to Sue, a tramp. Or even perhaps a lone camper who ran away because he did not want to be caught trespassing in the camp-owned shelter.

The hikers turned in early, rolling themselves up in the blankets they had brought, and the last thing Cherry saw was a canopy of stars; then she fell asleep.

The campers awoke to a bright blue sky. The air was filled with birdcalls. Jean Wheeler already had a hot fire going, and Katy, who must have been up before anyone, appeared with her bandanna full of wild red berries she had picked.

"Raspberries," Katy announced.

Sue washed the berries and helped Katy dish them up as a first course for breakfast. Jean Wheeler made a marvelous pancake mix; she poured the syrup and butter right into the batter. Each girl browned her own flapjacks, Cherry flipping hers as deftly as anyone.

After breakfast and cleanup, the girls went exploring. Sue said to Cherry, "I want to show you something."

"One of those tamarack trees we've been watching for?"

"No, this is something—maybe—about that man we saw yesterday."

Sue led Cherry to the spring, then beyond it to a sheltered area where a stream bubbled. There she held aside low-hanging branches and beckoned Cherry to follow.

"See it? I found it when I came for water this morning."

"This what you mean?"

It was a fishing rod made of a long, recently peeled, green branch and some sturdy twine. It lay on the bank with the twine tangled, as if its owner had flung the rod down in a hurry.

"Miss Cherry, notice the way the bark was whittled off this branch? In arrow-shaped strokes? That's the way Mac Cook whittled for us."

The rod could belong to Mac Cook. Cherry did not believe that he had gone to New York, not after seeing Fred Epler's jeep on the road when he wouldn't have had time to get back, not after what Reed Champion had observed at the station. If Mac had *not* gone to New York, if he still had some unfinished business here with Purdy, mightn't he be camping out—or hiding out—in these hills?

Cherry did not want to worry Sue. "We-ell, lots of people use a jackknife this way," was all she said.

Cherry knelt and examined the fishhook. It was a very good, new, commercial hook.

If the man were Mac Cook, how had he come by this fishhook? At the local hardware stores? No one had seen him in the town or village since he left suddenly last Saturday. Or had Mac kept the hook on hand against the day of his leaving Blue Water? But his flight from camp had been sudden, an emergency, probably unplanned—

"Sue, did you ever see Mac fishing at camp?"

"No, I never did."

The newspaper story came back to Cherry. The young cashier at the loan company, who was suspected of the robbery, had gone off on vacation on a camping trip and never returned. *On a camping trip.* That would account for the fishhook, for a camper often lives off the land.

Absently, Cherry pulled the red calico handkerchief out of her pocket. "Did you ever see this before, Sue?" she asked.

"Mac Cook had one like it. He tied it around his neck sometimes on very hot days. Where did you get it, Miss Cherry?"

"Found it in the shelter yesterday," Cherry said, still absently. Then she gathered her thoughts and added briskly, "But a lot of outdoor workers use these red calico handkerchiefs. Some of the men working at the Clemences' farm have them. Fred Epler has one. We can't be at all sure that this one is Mac's."

Cherry felt disturbed about the whole incident. If the furtive man they saw yesterday were Mac Cook, what was he up to, still hanging around this area?

Sue was worried and concerned for Mac. Cherry was surprised at her feelings.

"I'd hate to think it *is* Mac Cook," said Sue. "Why would he run from us? We're his friends—he was nice to us kids. Imagine if he's been camping out, all those rainy days! What's he using for supplies? I'll bet he's lonesome, too."

Cherry reiterated that the man might not be Mac, but Sue was inclined to believe it was.

Cherry really felt much the same way. She was debating whether, on their return, to report what they had found this morning, when Jean Wheeler's whistle blew.

"Time to pack up! Time to start back!" she called.

CHAPTER IX

Strange Story

~~~~~~~~~~~~~~~~~~~~~~~~~~~~~~~~~~~~~

AFTER THE DISCOVERY IN THE FOREST, SUE CON-
tinued to worry about Mac Cook. Cherry hinted that
Mac Cook—if the man were he—might or might
not be worth worrying about. But Sue would not
believe this, and reports from the boys, at the next
square dance, troubled her further. D. V. and his
cabin mates had been on an overnight hike Friday
and Saturday, immediately after the girls' return.
Though the boys had not gone to that particular
shelter, they, too, had discovered traces of someone
living in the wilderness.

At her first opportunity, Cherry talked to Reed
Champion about the matter. He knew the land, the
people, the habits around here. Reed had an idea.

"If we could find out that Mac *did* go to New
York, it would set Sue's mind at ease, right? Well,"
said Reed in that level tone of his, "it's more likely

Mac would take the train than hitchhike, if he was in such a hurry. Why don't we do this?—"

The head conductor on the one daily run between the nearest town and New York was Wilbur Hall. He was an old-time railroad man who knew affectionately every passenger, their children, grandchildren, and visitors, and their whole life histories; when he didn't know a passenger, Mr. Hall got acquainted with him right away. If Mac Cook had taken the train, Mr. Hall would be sure to know, or at the very least would hear about the new passenger from one of his train crew.

"There aren't many travelers on this local line, except camp people," Reed said, "so Mac Cook would stick out like a sore thumb."

Reed promised to inquire when he drove to town Monday on an errand. On Monday morning Cherry had occasion to walk to the village, and she asked at the drugstore, the waffle shop, the hardware store, the grocery store, the garage, for any news of Mac Cook. Not a soul had seen him nor heard of him in over a week.

When Cherry reported this much to her, Sue said:

"That means Mac, or whoever the man is, hasn't come to the village for supplies. How long can he live on fish and wild berries?"

"Indefinitely, if he's lucky," said Cherry, "and if the good weather holds."

It did not. The rains started again on Tuesday, in unseasonal downpours. The Clemences said that they and other local farmers were glad of the rain,

for the wells had been very low and needed re-
plenishing, but Fred Epler, bringing eggs to camp,
looked glum when Cherry saw him Tuesday. That
wasn't like Fred; he was generally cheerful.

Before Tuesday was over, Cherry realized she
had stirred up a tide of gossip with her questions
in the village about Mac Cook. In a country place,
gossip spread swiftly. It had reached the photographer, she found, who knocked at the door of the
Blue Water infirmary. In his wide, shapeless raincoat she did not recognize him at first.

"Oh, it's you, Mr. Purdy! Come in. Dr. and Mrs.
Lowell are having supper down the hill," Cherry
explained.

"I've hurt my hand and I am half drowned,"
the photographer grumbled, walking in. "These dark
wet days, not good days to be alone in one's house
or barn all day."

Cherry attended to the cut on Paul Purdy's hand,
unpleasant but not serious. He said the supplies
in his first-aid kit were stale; besides, he was awkward at bandaging his own hand. Purdy seemed
nervous and out of sorts.

"I do not like this talk of a man lurking in the
woods," he said to Cherry. "Ever since I heard it,
I have left the lights on all night in the barn—and
the house, too," he added hastily.

"My goodness, Mr. Purdy," said Cherry, "if you
keep something so valuable on your place, why don't
you ask for police protection?"

Purdy did not answer. He grumbled a little more,
then said he'd see if Bob Wright had time for a

chat. Well, Cherry thought, maybe "Pep" Purdy was just in a dark-blue mood and feeling rather jumpy from the rain.

Then Reed Champion telephoned from town. He had been able to catch Wilbur Hall for a couple of minutes when the train came through.

"Said he hadn't seen anyone answering to Mac Cook's description," Reed reported.

"The conductor *would* have seen him, surely, if he'd been on the train? Then Mac wasn't on the train—"

"Apparently not. Now the question is, where *did* he run off to? Or *did* he elude the conductor?"

They hung up, uncertain.

Like the pieces of a jigsaw puzzle, Cherry mused, these odd elements of information should suggest a design. But she could not fit them together. The key piece must be missing. What was that key? Was it Mac Cook? Cherry stared thoughtfully through the rain across the lake. Somewhere in those deserted hills a man hid, perhaps starved, and waited.

There was no question about it, Vernie Epler was on the edge of hysteria. She nearly jumped out of her skin when Cherry rapped on the screen door Wednesday morning, calling, "It's just me, in need of cream for another birthday party."

Vernie, admitting her, stumbled and upset the boiling water of the teakettle all over her own ankles and feet. Vernie could barely control the tears in her round blue eyes.

"Are you burned?" Cherry asked, quickly kneeling. "Let me see, Vernie. Sit down. Take off your stockings."

"I'm not burned," Vernie mumbled. "Yes, I am. Yes, I'd better sit down."

Cherry helped her hobble over to the rocking chair. She noticed how white Vernie was, how shallow her breathing. There was some degree of shock here. She saw hot coffee on the stove.

"Vernie, drink this, it will help you." Cherry poured a cup of hot black coffee for her, as a stimulant. Then she found two sweaters hanging on hooks and put these around the young farm wife. "I'm sorry I startled you so badly," she added.

"You didn't—it's just, oh, everything. Just me," Vernie said.

Vernie handed Cherry the emptied coffee cup. Her skin was regaining its normal color, but she grimaced with pain.

"I'm going to remove your stockings," Cherry told her. "Relax. I'll try to be very gentle."

Vernie kicked off her shoes. Cherry rolled down the stockings, going very slowly and carefully when she came to the scalded ankles and insteps. The skin revealed was a raw red and, Cherry could see, was going to blister. A second-degree burn, probably. The left stocking stuck. For a moment Cherry thought she would have to cut around the stocking, rather than pull and risk ripping the skin. But then the stocking gave of its own accord.

"There's absorbent cotton and iodine in the bathroom cabinet," Vernie said weakly.

"Never, on this deep a burn," Cherry cautioned

her. "Iodine burns, too, you know, and the cotton will stick."

"Well, then, you'll find butter in the churn—"

Cherry smiled up at the young woman. "Not butter, either. I don't want to alarm you, you'll be fine, but this isn't just a superficial burn."

Cherry asked for baking soda and sterile gauze and a large basin. Vernie was not sure she had any gauze in the house, but she had soft, clean white cloths in the linen drawer in the kitchen. Baking soda was in the cupboard.

"Good," said Cherry. "Now in just a minute, I'll make you more comfortable." And safe from infection, she added to herself. First, she thoroughly washed her hands with soap and hot water.

Vernie watched despondently while Cherry heated a basin full of fresh water to lukewarm, added two or three tablespoonfuls of baking soda, then soaked two clean white cloths in the soda solution. Twisting the ends of the cloths so they would not drip, Cherry applied the warm wet dressings to Vernie's feet and ankles.

"That feels better," Vernie sighed. "I'm so ashamed of myself, Miss Cherry. Nervous, I guess. I'm *never* so clumsy."

"Anybody can have an accident," Cherry soothed her.

She did not miss Vernie's hint that she was badly upset about something. But Cherry's first concern was medical care for her.

"Have you a phone so that I can call a doctor? Either our camp doctor, or your own?"

"I'd rather have Dr. Lowell."

Vernie said that they were on a party line, and the telephone was in the front hallway. When Cherry went to telephone the infirmary, she thought she heard a door open upstairs.

"Dr. Lowell will be over in an hour," Cherry said, returning to Vernie. "Too bad he can't come sooner, but it's all right as long as your husband keeps the dressings moist. Is Fred at home?"

"He's in the village," Vernie said unhappily.

Cherry sat down to wait. Vernie stared into space, brooding. A slight sound from upstairs made her grip the arms of the rocking chair. She looked guiltily toward Cherry and as quickly glanced away.

"Do you want to tell me what's worrying you, Vernie?" Cherry asked. "I want to help if I can."

"Believe me, you *do* help me, I appreciate it a whole lot. But—but I can't— Oh, it's nothing, honestly."

"I can't believe it's *nothing* that made you so upset you scalded yourself."

"Please, Miss Cherry, don't ask me to talk."

"Very well. I'll just saturate the dressing again—"

While she was doing so, footsteps sounded on the stairs. Vernie strained forward in her chair, her round face frightened. Then Mac Cook came in. He was freshly shaven, his mustache was gone. Mac looked tired and worn, and he had caught a cold. His yellow hair was brown at the roots.

"Hello, Miss Cherry. Surprised to see me? It's all right, Vernie. I've come to a decision."

Cherry was so surprised she was speechless. Mac Cook poured himself a cup of coffee. Vernie had started to cry soundlessly; Mac patted her on the shoulder.

"I heard Miss Cherry telephone for the doctor. Gee, I'm sorry you burned yourself. Is it bad?"

Vernie was unable to reply. Cherry said, "It's painful but she's not in any danger."

"I just had to come downstairs to see if you're all right. But listen, Vernie. I wasn't going to hide any more, anyway. I can't keep this up. It's what Fred has been warning me about all along. I have to tell somebody the truth! And Miss Cherry has been awfully decent to me.

"Look, Miss Cherry, no matter what you think, I'm no criminal. Don't look at me like that! I know I've done a lot of peculiar things but— Are you willing at least to listen to my story?"

"Yes, I'm always willing to listen."

Vernie said suddenly, "I'm glad you're going to tell the truth, after all these awful weeks! Maybe if a fair-minded person like Miss Cherry believes you, then you'll—"

"Maybe Miss Cherry will even help me," Mac said. "Telling the truth isn't going to be enough to solve the mystery."

"But now you *must* tell me the truth, Mac," Cherry said gently but firmly.

"So help me, I'll tell you the truth! My name is Jack Waldron. Mac Cook is just a name I made up. Though by this time even Vernie and Fred call me Mac. Fred Epler and I are half brothers."

"So that's it!" Cherry exclaimed. "I thought when I first came to Blue Water that you two men looked rather alike, but I didn't— Wait a minute! Jack Waldron is the name of a loan company cashier who's suspected of robbery."

"Yes. I'm the man who went off on vacation on a camping trip, and never came back. Because of Purdy. I can't tell you how—how bowled over I was to find Pep Purdy, of all people, around *here.*"

Cherry's head was reeling. "Maybe you'd better start telling your story at the beginning," she said.

"You were with me, Miss Cherry, when I first saw Purdy around here—that day at the Model Farm's greenhouse, remember?" Mac Cook—or rather, Jack Waldron—smiled a curious smile. "All right, I'll begin at the beginning."

He told a strange story. It dated back to when he was three years old, when his father died. His young mother soon married again. Fred was born a year later when Mac was four. Mrs. Epler tried to be a good mother to both boys, but she never regained her full strength after a siege of pneumonia. Mr. Epler found a home for them all with a family which had its own children, but where Mrs. Epler would get proper care. In the crowded house, Mac was—or he felt—neglected, perhaps because Fred, who was younger, required more attention. Sometimes, in his unhappiness as he grew up, he was difficult. By the time he was eleven, his step-father threatened to place him in an orphanage whenever Mac misbehaved.

Somehow, throughout all this strain at home, Fred and Mac managed to be loyal friends. Fred looked up to his older half brother, and Mac always cared for and looked out for the younger boy.

Then their mother died, and Jacob Epler did place Mac, at twelve, in an orphanage. After paying Mac a few halfhearted visits, Mr. Epler moved away and took Fred with him. Mac did not see or hear of his stepfather and half brother again.

He was trained in the orphanage to earn his own living, and graduated at eighteen. Then Mac made his way alone. He had always been a lonely person, and despite a few friendships he remained so. He did not marry. He was not sure whether Fred would want to see him again, even after the orphanage authorities told him that Mr. Epler had died.

He had one lead about where to find Fred. An old uncle in Mr. Epler's family had owned a small farm in northeastern Pennsylvania, which would eventually belong to Mr. Epler and then to Fred. Mr. Epler had boasted a great deal about the farm and had taken the boys to visit it one time. Little Fred and Mac had talked about and dreamed about the farm when they were children. Mac never forgot it.

"That's why, when I was in trouble," he said to Cherry and Vernie, "and didn't have a soul to help me, I headed for this farm."

"What sort of trouble?"

"You think I robbed the loan company, don't you? So do the police. They're looking for me."

Cherry stiffened. She looked inquiringly toward Vernie. This time Vernie looked straight back at her.

"Fred and I wouldn't harbor a criminal, Miss Cherry. Half brother or no half brother, we just don't do things like that!"

"Now wait, wait," Mac pleaded, "before you judge me. Let me tell you the facts about Purdy."

"I don't see what a photographer has to do with the loan company robbery," Cherry said doubtfully. "The newspapers didn't even mention his name."

"Sure they didn't. Oh, Purdy's a clever one! I wish I'd never met that man."

Mac had run into Pep at a quiet little restaurant in New York City where both of them ate their dinners regularly every evening. Presently the photographer spoke to Mac and struck up an acquaintance. He told Mac that he was a photographer, and showed Mac some of his commercial pictures which were signed Pep. He never told Mac that his full name was Paul E. Purdy; he avoided giving Mac his address. Once or twice he casually mentioned his cottage somewhere in the country not far from New York; Mac got the impression that it was in Connecticut.

Mac was grateful for the man's companionship. He was too sensitive about his unhappy past to talk about that, or about his half brother and the farm, so Mac kept the conversation in the present, and quite naturally told the photographer his name and the name of the loan company where he worked.

"I didn't need to tell Purdy," Mac said dryly. "He already knew, he *must* have, that's why he spoke to me in the first place. But he didn't let on, and I didn't figure out the truth until it was too late. He seemed like such a nice man."

Gradually, over their dinners, Pep confided to Mac that his photography studio was not doing very well. He needed money, soon, pretty urgently. He half joked about his troubles, as if embarrassed. He teased Mac about the big sums of currency a cashier handled every day, and, not at all incidentally, he pumped the lonely, unsuspecting young man for certain information: the layout of the office; where the bulk of the money was kept; on what days and hours the largest sums were in the loan company office, when business was rushing and the most clients were around.

"One evening, just before my vacation, which I'd mentioned was coming," Mac said, "Pep made another joke about all that money lying around at the loan company. He said it ought to be no trouble at all for a fellow to help himself to some of it. Well, I didn't think that joke was so funny."

"You see, Miss Cherry," Vernie said earnestly, "he was trying to get Mac to go in with him on the robbery. Mac's already told Fred and me the whole thing," she added.

"Yes, I see," said Cherry.

"Oh, Pep insisted he was only joking as usual. When he saw I didn't go for his idea, he just laughed it off and didn't mention it again. But I realized he'd led me into talking too much."

Very soon after this, Mac had left on vacation, starting off alone on his camping trip. He had been gone a little more than a week when the story of the robbery broke in all the newspapers and radio newscasts.

"The first I heard of it was when I bought a New York newspaper on Saturday, June fifteenth, in some little mountain burg—and I read that *I* was suspected of doing the job just the day before! Why, it was next to impossible! I was camping and fishing in the woods by myself all that week! Try and prove it, though! I had no alibi. Well, the first thing I thought of was Pep's joke about robbing the loan company. But according to the newspapers, nobody suspected *him*—they suspected me."

Mac was so stunned that all he could do was take cover and try to think what to do next. If he went back to his job, he would be taken into custody, on charges of robbery, and probably locked up. He had only a little money with him; besides, a hunted man could not camp out indefinitely.

"I didn't know which way to turn—didn't know whether I had a friend left in the world—and Fred is all the family I've got. So I decided to look up my half brother. Secretly. By back roads. We'd been good friends as kids, I figured I could talk things over with Fred. Maybe he'd know what to do, or maybe he'd at least help me to hide out for a while. What I hoped was that the police would catch the thief pretty quickly."

"And you think the thief is Purdy?"

"Wouldn't you, Miss Cherry? You see what Purdy did, don't you?"

"No, I don't," Cherry said.

"Purdy waited for a few days after I'd gone. Then, on June fourteenth, he dressed himself up in that big, loose raincoat of his—he and I are about the same height, five feet six, and in that raincoat you can't see whether Purdy is plump, or slim like me. Besides the flowing raincoat, he pulled his hatbrim down low, and used a rubber mask."

Cherry caught her breath. "You mean the mask I found in the lake? But how do I know it wasn't *you* who threw the mask in the lake?"

"If *I'd* thrown the mask in the lake, why would I want it back? Why, asking for it back would only throw suspicion on me," Mac pointed out.

"The mask isn't proof," Cherry told Mac gently.

"I know. I wanted the mask to find out if it was the same kind of mask I'd seen in his barn as a prop—to make sure in my own mind whether he'd framed me!"

Cherry accepted this explanation but another question arose. Why had Purdy—if it had been Purdy—gone to all the trouble of rowing out to the middle of the lake to dispose of the mask? He could have destroyed it in other ways. Yes, but did a man in panic, as Purdy might well have been after his barn was invaded—did he think rationally of all the possibilities? Cherry remembered that even the most cunning of criminals always make at least one mistake which sooner or later is their undoing.

She concluded that Purdy chose the lake in a moment of panic for getting rid of the mask.

"You aren't listening to me," Mac said. "Please listen. This is important—"

In their conversations at dinner Mac had used his pet expression, "Great balls of fire!" Mac insisted now that Purdy had deliberately used those words to make the two women employees believe he was Mac.

"It's plausible," Cherry said, "and I'm inclined to believe you. But the police would say it's still possible that you sneaked back from vacation, in disguise, and robbed the safe. And that you could be trying to pin the blame on Purdy. Isn't that true?"

She waited. There was no answer.

"If you're innocent, Mac," Cherry said, "why haven't you gone to the police?"

Vernie said something confused and distressed; it was lost. Mac ran his hands through his streaked hair. Then he painfully explained:

When he was in his teens, he had gone along for a ride with some young friends of his. Mac did not know, when he accepted the ride, that one boy, for a prank, had stolen a car. The police had recovered the abandoned car and picked up one boy who talked. Though Mac had not taken the car, he had always felt guilty about the episode and still did not feel easy about approaching the police now. It made him uncomfortable that the incident might be uncovered. The whole moral question worried him a great deal.

There was a ring of truth and regret in what he said, Cherry admitted to herself. Even without this incident in his past, Mac might well want proof of his innocence before he returned to his job—or went to the police who suspected him.

"You want proof against Purdy, Miss Cherry? I believe the proof of his guilt, and my innocence, is right there in his storage barn. I'll tell you why I think so—"

"Then you *are* the one who broke into his barn!"

"Yes," Mac said, unblinking. "I *have* to get the proof."

"Is that connected with why you moved from here to the Model Farm, and then moved to Blue Water?"

"I moved from here because I didn't want to involve Fred and Vernie any deeper. They were good to me, took me in."

Vernie said, "We urged Mac to go to the police right away, and report how Mr. Purdy had wanted him to collaborate. But Mac kept pleading with us for time to think."

"I had to think how I might track Purdy down, and clear myself," Mac explained to Cherry. "But as far as *staying* with Fred and Vernie, why, it wasn't fair to them! I didn't want any suspicion cast on *them*."

Mac realized that the police would check the histories of all loan company employees, past and present. If the police investigations led to Mac's half brother, he didn't want the Eplers involved by being found at their house.

"That's why I went to work at the Model Farm. I had only a few dollars left to exist on, and I was unable to get out what little money I have in a New York bank. I wouldn't live off Fred, and I didn't have enough money to return to New York to trace Purdy, or keep watch on him. All I knew was that I needed time to think, and a job to live on, and I wanted to keep in touch with Fred. Then, you remember, Miss Cherry, that day at the Model Farm—"

"Purdy showed up at the greenhouse, to your surprise, and you—"

"—realized that with Purdy living around here, I had a—it was almost like a miracle—a chance to find a way to clear myself."

It was then that Mac decided to search Purdy's barn for the proof he felt sure must be there. The Model Farm was an awkward distance from Purdy's, so Mac got himself a job at Camp Blue Water, which was very close to Purdy and his barn.

"Then this is why you dodged Purdy at every turn—why you fled when Purdy was within inches of meeting you! But when did you dye your hair and change your name?"

"As soon as I got here to Fred's. I had to disguise myself, until I could get hold of proof that I'm innocent."

Mac still needed to get that proof. On his first invasion of the barn he failed to find what he was after. After that, Purdy hardly ever left his place. He had placed heavy locks on the doors and windows, and he kept all the lights burning.

"Well, I figured I had to keep on trying to get into that barn until I *did* find proof. When Camp Blue Water became too unsafe for me, I hid in the woods waiting for my chance to try again."

"We found your fishing rod and your red calico handkerchief," Cherry said.

Mac nodded in a despairing way. "I can't go on living like this. It's just a stroke of luck that the police haven't come here so far."

"That night when the state police whizzed by, siren wailing," Cherry said, "and you ran for all you were worth—"

"I'd been down at the lake's edge with Fred— it wasn't fair to keep going to his house—discussing what I ought to do. Sure, when I heard the siren, I thought the police had come for me, and I ran. This isn't fair to Fred and Vernie, either. I'm about ready to give myself up, even with the proof a stone's throw away." His voice trembled. "Hiding out in the hills, in all that rain—it was pretty awful. I would have starved if Fred and Vernie hadn't given me food when I came over here twice in the middle of the night."

"Last night, Miss Cherry," Vernie said, "he came to us. We made him stay the night with us. We saw he was half sick, and at his wit's end—"

"You didn't have to persuade me much, Vernie. I'm— I guess I'm at the end of my rope. I have no hope left."

Cherry was stirred. Suppose this young man were innocent—suppose proof actually existed in Purdy's barn? She recalled how nervous Purdy was about his barn, and, above all, how he had refused to ask for police protection.

"What *is* the proof, Mac?"

"Why, it's the money Purdy took from the loan company, of course! Haven't you noticed that the newspaper reports didn't say a word about it?"

"That's right. Apparently the money hasn't turned up anywhere," Cherry said. "But what makes you so sure it's in Purdy's barn?"

"Because Purdy wouldn't be such a fool as to try to spend or deposit that money until after the case cools off. He's a clever man."

They heard the jeep driving in very fast, too fast, brake to a sharp stop.

Fred burst into the kitchen. "I just saw Purdy at the garage—trying to borrow something—I don't know what, but the garageman was pretty sore! I tell you, Purdy's up to something!"

Then Fred saw Cherry. "A friend, I hope?"

"Yes," said Cherry. "Now let's see what we can plan. I have an idea."

CHAPTER X

Cherry Lends a Hand

"I CAN'T IMAGINE WHAT'S BECOME OF MAC," SUE fretted. It was early Thursday morning and Sue, counting back, figured, "It's six days since we saw that man running in the forest, and it's nearly two weeks since Mac ran away from Blue Water."

Cherry pretended to concentrate on pinning her white starched cap to her black curls. She wished she could tell Sue that she had seen Mac Cook only yesterday at the Eplers'. Sue caught her eye in the cabin mirror.

"Aren't *you* worried about him, Miss Cherry?"

"There's plenty to be worried about," Cherry admitted.

She thought to herself that Sue would be still more concerned about Mac if she knew about the danger he was in.

The girls' camp was at breakfast when Reed Champion drove in to see Uncle Bob Wright. A traveling circus was coming to town, and Reed was on his way to purchase tickets for the two camps. He had stopped to check on the number of tickets needed.

Reed caught up with Cherry for a moment at the Mess Hall door.

"Are you going to be free this evening? There's a chance—just a chance—of some of us going over to Tall Man's Island for a picnic supper." Reed smiled. "Now that the summer is nearly over, Thunder Cliff is running like clockwork. That's how I can get away."

The same thing was true at Blue Water, Cherry told him; the infirmary was completely idle. "I'd love to see Tall Man's Island."

"Well, it's a *maybe*. So long for now."

Cherry waved to him as he drove off but she was not thinking of Reed Champion. Her mind was on Mr. Paul E. Purdy, with whom she had some special business today.

The plan was simple—the plan which she, Mac Cook, and the Eplers had decided on—simple and dangerous. What Mac had to do, now that he had tracked down Purdy, was to prove Purdy's guilt. Evidence, he felt sure, was in Purdy's barn. But Mac dared not let Purdy catch sight of him; Mac would remain in hiding upstairs in the Eplers' farmhouse.

Fred Epler was willing to make some contact with Purdy, but there was a risk that the photographer, with his trained vision, might observe the likeness between Fred and the young loan company cashier, even though he apparently had not noticed it yet. Still, they didn't want to take any chances, and since Vernie had declared she was afraid of Purdy, that left Cherry as the only go-between. Purdy would not link her in any way with the Eplers or Mac Cook or with the robbery in New York.

Cherry's job was to pay a call on Mr. Purdy and try to look for the money or to trap him into revealing some information. She went as early as she decently could, Dr. Lowell excusing her. There was no point in going too early, for the neighborhood knew Purdy was a night owl and a late riser.

At ten o'clock she knocked on the door of Pep Purdy's cottage. No one answered. The door was locked, the windows were opened only a few inches and made immovable by safety catches. All the lights in the house were on, in broad daylight.

"Purdy must really be nervous," Cherry thought, "and maybe growing peculiar." She walked through the small orchard to his barn, whistling and stepping on crackling twigs so that Purdy would hear her coming. She did not want to surprise him and raise a barrier of mistrust, or incur his resentment. She still did not really know whether Purdy was a dangerous man, as Mac insisted, but she was going to be cautious.

The barn door was locked and the barn windows were dark. Cherry peered in but saw no signs of life inside. That was puzzling and discouraging. She sat down on the grass, out of the August sun, prepared to wait as long as necessary. She would be careful not to mention Mac Cook, whom Purdy apparently still had never quite caught a glimpse of in this area, nor mention the Eplers.

At once she heard the door bolt being opened from the inside. The barn door opened part way and the photographer emerged. He was not glad to have a visitor.

"You here again, Miss Nurse?" He half closed the barn door so that she could not see in. "Would you be so good as to explain why you were looking in my barn window?"

"Just looking around for you, Mr. Purdy. I'm sorry if I intruded." She wondered what he had been doing in the darkened barn, but Purdy was quicker than she.

"I was developing some films," he said. "I have a darkroom in my barn, you see."

"How convenient," Cherry said politely. "Isn't it a hot day? Your barn probably is the coolest place around here. The girls at Blue Water were wishing they had a cooler place to rehearse in, you know they're—"

Purdy turned away, bored and annoyed. Cherry talked resolutely on.

"—getting ready for their final show of the season, the water pageant. I came over to ask you about costumes and—"

"Yes, yes, costumes, props, of course I will lend them. Now if you will excuse me, Miss Nurse. I am busy this morning."

"Busy with your films?" Cherry boldly followed him into the barn.

He did not let her enter beyond a step or two.

Nevertheless, in that instant, Cherry took a sweeping look at the barn's shadowy contents. What was that low, square object over which Purdy had thrown his very full raincoat? It seemed to be firm in outline, propping up the raincoat in a vague oblong. Could it be an overnight case in which Purdy might have concealed the stolen money?

"Really, Miss Nurse, we can discuss the costumes some other time."

"This afternoon?" Cherry pressed.

"No, not this afternoon!"

Purdy said it so sharply that Cherry jumped. Immediately he was all blandness.

"Yes, yes, perhaps this afternoon, if you wish. But tomorrow would be much better for me. Shall we say sometime tomorrow?"

"I'd give a lot to know," thought Cherry, *"what you're up to this afternoon?"* But aloud she said, "Tomorrow will be fine, Mr. Purdy. Thanks ever so much." And she walked away.

"But I'll be back this afternoon," she vowed to herself.

Cherry returned to camp, to allow a little time to pass and to report in at the infirmary. There really was nothing for her or the Lowells to do. The three of them sat on the porch and talked about the possibility of paddling over to Tall Man's Island that night. The nurse from Camp Thunder Cliff was willing to take charge of their infirmary for the evening. Cherry was glad to hear that Vernie Epler's scalded ankles were healing. Dr. Lowell said he was satisfied, after treating Vernie, that the burn was under control—thanks to Cherry's prompt action.

Cherry had an odd sense of remoteness during lunch. The girls around her chatted of the final swimming tests which Ruth J. was conducting during this next-to-last week of camp—about the circus they and Thunder Cliff would attend tomorrow— of the coming water pageant which would be the camp season's grand finale. Sue wanted to be sixteen and a Water Queen; Katy, more modest now in her demands, said she'd just be one of the dolphins. To Cherry their lighthearted talk seemed far away, yet it reminded her that the summer, and time to help Mac, were fast running out.

Right after lunch, Cherry took an inconspicuous hilly back trail for the short walk to Purdy's. She carried a tin pail and had ready some remarks about berrying.

Stopping behind a screen of willow trees, she surveyed his place.

No one was on Purdy's grounds; no lights burned in Purdy's house or barn. Was he out? Or was he locked in the darkened barn again, "developing films.". . . It took courage for Cherry to go rap on the barn door and call. There was no answer, not a sound disturbed the quiet of the summer afternoon. She searched the orchard, then tried the locked house door. Not a sound here, either, except the breeze stirring in the apple trees.

"Did I scare Purdy off this morning? No, I don't think so. Whatever he was planning, he must have decided before I got there, for he was so determined not to see me this afternoon."

Where had he gone? Cherry walked around to the garage built at one side of the cottage. This, too, was locked. By standing on tiptoe she could see Purdy's car inside. If he were headed for New York, or going any distance, he would have taken his car. This probably meant Purdy was somewhere not far away.

Then Cherry noticed unmistakable footprints. In the damp or muddy spots under trees, which still had not dried out after all the rains, lay the blunt imprints of Purdy's rope-soled sandals. Cherry followed these to the highway.

Now where? Across the highway? That would lead into a deep thicket which went down to the lake.

Cherry pushed into the thicket of trees, watching the ground at every step. Yes, here were Purdy's footprints, going toward the water. But here and there, along with the footprints, Cherry caught sight of a small, deep, square mark. She bent down. It looked like the corner of something, as if Purdy had been carrying a box and rested it at intervals.

The footprints led to the water's edge, and then there was nothing.

Had a boat been moored here? Cherry searched in the tall grasses for a stake and rope, or a heavy rock, or wooden wedge. But she could not find a thing. She recalled hearing that Purdy cared little for fishing and rowing, and had not bothered to replace his rowboat when it got waterlogged one summer.

No boat. Then had he stepped off into the water

to go swimming? Not likely, with his sandals on and carrying a heavy object. Unless— For a few minutes Cherry beat through the greenery, searching for his sandals or anything left or hidden there. But there was no trace of Purdy, no hint of his destination.

"He *must* have left by boat," Cherry thought. "Did he borrow one from a neighbor? Or did someone—possibly an accomplice—come for him?"

She could not do any more here or by herself. The next step was to get help. Half running, Cherry raced back to camp, to telephone. She wanted to talk to Fred Epler, and possibly Reed, too, could help her. There was a telephone she might use with some privacy in the Main House.

Ruth J. was coming out of the Main House, a beach coat thrown over her bathing suit. She was very much annoyed.

"Someone has swiped one of our rowboats," she told Cherry. "When we need every single boat for our water skills tests! I just reported it to Bob Wright. He thinks whoever did it probably helped himself while we were all at lunch." Ruth J. hurried off.

"Purdy," Cherry thought. "He could easily have taken the back hillside trail, cut through the deserted cabin area to the water front, and rowed a boat away to his place." No one in the Mess Hall could have seen him on the water, because of the trees which grew luxuriantly along the lake's edge. Then he could have left the boat there while he went to get the box or whatever it was that he was carrying.

Cherry reached Fred Epler by telephone. Speaking guardedly because it was a party line, she reported what had happened. She could hear Fred Epler relaying her words to Mac and Vernie. Fred came on the telephone again.

"You know what this means, don't you, Miss Cherry? It means he could be on his way to *any one* of the islands down Long Lake! There are a lot of them. He may feel that one of them would be safer than his barn, if you know what I mean."

"I know," Cherry said. "Fred, which island would you guess?"

"Well, the farthest one away and the most deserted is Tall Man's Island. It's wild, and that's where I'd head in a pinch."

Cherry said, "Listen, Fred. I think I can go over to Tall Man's Island this evening . . . What? . . . No, with some of the counselors.". . . Fred Epler wanted to come along. "And risk giving the whole situation away?" Cherry said. "No, just let me go and have a look."

"Will there be some men in the party?" Fred was anxious to know.

"How brave do you think I am?" Cherry asked, laughing.

Next, Cherry called Reed at Thunder Cliff. She told him that though she could not disclose the reason by telephone, it was urgent for their picnic to take place that evening.

Good friend that he was, Reed answered, "Sure thing. We'll go."

CHAPTER XI

Night Watch

THE PICNICKERS STARTED OFF EARLY, AT SIX P.M., while there was still plenty of daylight. A birthday party for two of the Midgets was in full swing, and Cherry thought she could slip out of camp without arousing Sue's curiosity. But Sue had seen Cherry looking worried all day today, dashing in and out of camp.

"*Now*, where are you going, Miss Cherry?" Sue asked. She was holding a flower-crowned Midget by the hand, and wore a paper clown's cap on her own head. "Something's up. I know it is!"

"Oh, some of us are going on a picnic to Tall Man's Island," Cherry said. "The Lowells—" She waved toward the Lowells, to whom Sophie was handing a basket of lunch. "And Reed, Leona Jackson, Ruth J., and two Thunder Cliff counselors."

"Huh!" Sue looked at Cherry skeptically. "Why are you going all the way to the far end of Long

Lake for a picnic? It'll be dark by the time you paddle way down there."

"That's why I'm in a hurry," Cherry fibbed. " 'By now—"

"But you haven't told me—"

"I'll tell you when I can, Sue. Honestly. Now I have to run."

Reed and the two other young men were already waiting at the water front. They decided to take three canoes. Leona Jackson climbed in with the Lowells and the lunch. Ruth J. and the two Thunder Cliff counselors shared the second canoe. Reed and Cherry took the third, and swung out on the water as the lead boat.

The lake was glassy smooth. Once past Thunder Cliff, unbroken banks of trees lined their way. Birds flew overhead. Laughter carried from the other canoes. But Cherry was in a serious mood and Reed felt it.

"What's bothering you, Cherry? Why did you call me and say the picnic had to be this evening?"

"Reed, so much has happened since I saw you last. I'm convinced now that Mac Cook is innocent, and I think we may find the—the man who has framed him on Tall Man's Island."

Reed stared. "Who is the man? Do you know him?"

"Yes, and you know him, too. It's the photographer, Paul Purdy."

"Purdy—of all people!" Reed paddled faster. "We'd better try to get to the island before it's dark."

Air and water turned sapphire blue as they

skimmed along. The lake opened out, wider and lonelier. Islands began to loom up, and wild coves, where only birdcalls broke the stillness. But Cherry and Reed noticed little of this, for Cherry was telling Reed all that she had learned. After the sun set, about seven thirty, Reed asked Cherry to switch on her flashlight, as a taillight for the other two boats to follow.

Dusk was closing in when they saw the dim, solitary outlines of Tall Man's Island. Its trees made a tall, dense, dark silhouette. Cherry thought she could see something like matches being struck on the island, or was it fireworks?

"Don't you see that shower of sparks, Reed? Quite near the shore, up where the shore curves."

"Might be fireflies." He was more concerned with nosing the canoe safely through the rocks which reached out into the lake.

"It's too big and steady to be fireflies. It's like sparks shooting off a pinwheel or sparklers. It's as bright as an electric flash."

Reed looked, too. "That's not fireworks. Not an ordinary fire, either. Ordinary sparks fly upward, and these sparks shoot *down*. Say, what is that?"

He called to the others to look sharp for a landing, and began himself to hunt for a spot. Tall grasses and gnarled roots clogged their way. They came to a small U-shaped inlet.

"This will do," Reed said. "This is a natural."

"Reed," said Cherry, watching something else. "Those sparks—or whatever it is—they've stopped."

"Do you want to explore?"

They came to a small U-shaped inlet

"Yes. Please. Let's not tell the others, though."

"Okay. Beam the flashlight on the roots."

Reed stepped out, helped Cherry out, and pulled the canoe up on shore. The other two canoes pulled into the same inlet. "I'm starved!" Jan Lowell cried, and a babble of voices and scraping sounds disturbed the island's quiet.

But from where the sparks had blazed came a profound silence and shadows.

"He's heard us," Cherry realized. "Purdy, or whoever he is."

She and Reed told the others they'd collect firewood while the picnic lunch was being unpacked. They headed toward the spot where the sparks had flashed. Yellow sparks . . .

Cherry sniffed. Did she smell something like ether? She followed the faint sweetish odor, Reed close at her heels, and walked into a clearing. It was near the water's edge, yet shielded by trees.

"Someone has been here," Reed said. In the twilight they could make out flattened grasses where someone had trod. "Smell that?"

"But why ether?" Cherry puzzled. "Whoever he was, he must have known the sparks could be seen from the water."

"But he didn't expect anyone to come way out here," Reed answered. "I'd say he stayed close to the shore because he was working with something highly combustible and might need water in a hurry."

"Working with *what?*"

Cherry scanned the ground, using her flashlight, but could not see any clear prints in the grassy ground. Reed quietly told her to turn off the flashlight; it gave away their exact location. The man— or men?—might be watching them.

"I smell wood smoke, too," Reed muttered.

They pushed their way soundlessly toward a wisp of smoke, to find themselves looking down at the remains of a fire which had been splashed, apparently with lake water, only minutes ago.

"Where is he?" Cherry whispered.

"Either hiding deeper in the island, or he's escaped out on the water. Let's see if we can locate his boat."

They were several yards above the point where they themselves had landed, and around a curve. A few paces ahead, they came upon a deep, sheltered inlet. Reed knelt and picked up a length of rope.

It meant a rowboat had been here. The broken grasses were mute testimony, too. But had the boat been shoved out into the water? Or dragged and hidden among the bushes? They searched: no boat was secreted just here.

"Do you think he might have a gun?" Reed asked.

"I don't know." Cherry felt afraid for the first time. "What are you thinking?"

"That if we go out on the water looking for him, we'll be an easy target to shoot at. Also, he's had a head start. He could be waiting for us in his boat farther up the shore line."

"Or hiding right here on the island. We'll never

find him, now that it's growing dark," Cherry said.

Proof, Mac Cook had said. *The stolen money is the proof*. If we can find it—

"Let's not try to find him," Cherry urged. "Let's hunt for what he may have left behind, in his hurry."

"And for whatever made the sparks," Reed agreed.

It was hard to search in a shadowy forest at this hour. Reed covered the flashlight with Cherry's scarf; this done, they permitted themselves an instant's ray of light, here, there, ahead. The sound of singing—the picnickers'—came to them in gusts on the breeze.

"Isn't this freshly turned earth?" Reed asked, where a giant tree barred their way.

"He might have buried the money," Cherry thought aloud.

But neither she nor Reed, digging with their hands, could find anything. The earth might have been turned by groundhogs, they decided. They searched further, groping now. Scarcely able to see each other, Cherry and Reed linked hands to avoid getting separated. They were back again somewhere near the doused fire.

"What's that?" Cherry said sharply. Her flashlight beam, probing among the bushes, had picked up a hand. A man's hand. It did not stir.

She and Reed stood still in the darkness, waiting for any sound, any movement. Reed took the flashlight away from her.

"All right, come out of there!" Reed barked—so fiercely that Cherry jumped. "I've got you covered! Come out of there!"

It was sheer bluff. Did the man know it? He did not move or reply. Reed pulled the scarf away from the flashlight and turned the beam on full. He was taking a big chance, Cherry thought. Reed yanked her away as, simultaneously, he set the lighted flashlight on a stump. Cherry and Reed moved to one side of it.

The hand clutched at a bush. An arm appeared, and the man sat up, blinking in the beam. It was Purdy.

"I can't very well get up," he said. "I've hurt my foot. Where— I can't see you. You're camp people, aren't you? Lucky for me you came out here. Were you looking for me?"

"No, just picnicking," Cherry said untruthfully, since she did not want to arouse his suspicions.

Reed moved forward, picked up the flashlight, and ran its beam over the length of Purdy's body. Purdy's face was smudged and scared. Sure enough, his foot was badly burned. Fire or sparks had eaten away part of his sock and canvas rope-soled shoe. The foot beneath looked very sore, far worse than Vernie's scald.

"Better take a look at it, Cherry," said Reed. He held the flashlight for her. "You're lucky we have a nurse here, Purdy."

Cherry distastefully moved face to face with Pep Purdy. She examined the foot, being careful not to touch it. It looked like a third-degree burn; Dr. Lowell would have to see it at once. What struck Cherry was that the burn was fresh—it must have happened within the last few hours. Certainly she could not believe that Purdy with an injured foot had lugged the box, whose imprint she had found near his place, then rowed all the way to this island. No, Purdy must have had an accident to his foot right here.

"How did this happen, Mr. Purdy?" Cherry asked.

"I did it while I was building a fire. I am not a great outdoors man."

"I can't really believe that burn was caused by a little bonfire!" Cherry said to herself.

The photographer added shrewdly, "Since I was having trouble with the fire, I doused it, you see."

"We saw sparks," Reed said. "That's how you burned yourself, isn't it? What were you doing— using?"

"My dear boy, what nonsense!"

"I wish you'd tell us, so we'd know how to treat this burn," Cherry said.

But Purdy insisted he had brought no camping equipment except matches, a blanket, and sandwiches. He said that his boat was moored out of sight just above the U-shaped inlet where they had landed.

"Why didn't you call for help?" Reed demanded. "You surely heard us moving around."

Cherry nudged Reed to keep still. Nothing would be gained by antagonizing Purdy. She stood up, leaned over Purdy, and offered him her hand.

"We'll help you up. Dr. Lowell is here on the picnic, too, luckily for you."

"Oh, I am very, very lucky," said Purdy.

He made a pretext of leaning on Cherry but

she noticed that he could stand fairly well. Couldn't get up, indeed! He'd hoped that by crouching, they would not find him.

It was difficult for Purdy to walk, though. Reed and Cherry led him slowly in the direction of the picnickers. Cherry was reasonably sure he had brought a box of some sort to the island, yet he limped away with them, without so much as a glance around.

"If he's not worried about his box," Cherry figured, "that means he's probably got it in a safe place. Maybe hidden or buried right here where we surprised him—though would he have had time to *bury* it?"

The Lowells and the other counselors were surprised to see three persons reappear when they had expected only two—especially surprised to see their neighbor, the photographer. Cherry and Reed gave no sign that anything extraordinary or suspicious was happening. For that matter, they had found no clear-cut evidence that Purdy was *not* simply on a camping trip.

Dr. Lowell looked at the photographer's foot and pronounced it a third-degree burn. "We'll have to take you back to the infirmary as quickly as possible. Sorry I haven't any medical supplies with me. How did you burn yourself so badly, Mr. Purdy?"

Purdy ventured a laugh. "This is what I get for trying to become a camper like my Blue Water friends. Perhaps this is what a short man gets for visiting Tall Man's Island."

As urbane, as neighborly as ever! If Cherry had

not heard Mac Cook's story, and observed what she had about Purdy and his barn, well, she would still have trusted Purdy as unquestioningly as the others did.

Reed found Purdy's rowboat where he had described its mooring—only the boat was not Purdy's. It was the one which had been missing that afternoon. Ruth J. exclaimed when she saw it, by the light of their campfire and several flashlights. Purdy apologized. By now he was beginning to show exhaustion as a result of the burn, so Ruth J. forbore to scold him about the "borrowed" rowboat. Cherry and Reed managed to keep their faces expressionless during this byplay.

"Try to rest on the row home," Dr. Lowell told Purdy as they helped him into the borrowed boat. Reed would row Purdy; the doctor and Cherry would accompany them in a canoe. The others decided to stay and enjoy their picnic.

It was a long, silent trip home in the moonlight. The two craft rode nearly side by side. Cherry could hear no talk from Purdy, only curt answers when Reed occasionally spoke to him.

When they reached camp, the photographer, assisted by the doctor and Reed, hobbled the short distance to the infirmary. There Reed left them, taking the Thunder Cliff nurse back with him. Purdy was still closemouthed. Dr. Lowell, of course, suspected nothing. He did not urge his patient to talk. Assisted by Cherry, he cleansed and treated the burned foot, then gave the photographer a mild sedative.

Purdy revived with surprising speed. Cherry noted this a bit uneasily. Not that she wished Purdy any harm, but Reed had whispered something to her about "Keep him under surveillance tonight at his house"—then Reed had gone off in a hurry. Apparently he had some plan.

"I'll hear about it later," Cherry thought. "I'm glad Reed is on hand to help."

Dr. Lowell asked Cherry to drive Purdy back to his house. She did not enjoy being sent out on the roads alone with Purdy, but Dr. Lowell had no reason to know this, and Cherry could not tell him.

The doctor saw them settled in the jeep, and Cherry started off, going slowly. Purdy, beside her, sat stiff and hostile. She was glad the entrance to Camp Blue Water was well lighted, illuminating this stretch of road as well. The jeep had powerful headlights. Light was always a protection.

Suddenly Purdy came to life, tensed up. He was staring straight ahead. "Who's that?"

Down the road came a young man. The jeep's headlights picked up his odd brown-and-yellow hair. Squinting in the headlights' glare, he waved at Cherry—evidently not seeing who rode with her.

"Who's that?" Purdy asked under his breath. "I haven't seen that fellow around here before."

"I don't know him," Cherry drove past Mac, not even looking in his direction.

"He waved to you, didn't he?" Purdy asked.

"I don't know every farm hand around here," Cherry replied curtly.

She felt very nervous. Purdy had turned around and must be able to see Mac Cook's figure outlined by the lights at the camp's entrance. Why, oh why, hadn't Mac remained out of sight at the Eplers' house?

Cherry glanced at Purdy. Had he recognized Mac Cook? It was possible that he had. There had been twenty or thirty well-lighted seconds—on the other hand, Mac in his rough work clothes and odd hair didn't look like the man Purdy knew in New York as Jack Waldron. There was no telling from Purdy's sullen silence whether he had recognized Mac or not—whether he guessed Cherry and Mac were friends.

Reed and two of his counselors waited outside Purdy's house, standing beside the Thunder Cliff truck. That was a relief. Reed must have recruited his guards quickly, while she and Dr. Lowell treated Purdy in the infirmary.

"All right, Mr. Purdy, we'll help you into the house," Reed said. It was said in such a way as to avert Purdy's suspicion, but Purdy did not like all this attention.

"Thank you, I can manage." Purdy brushed aside Reed's proffered arm and limped quite rapidly to his cottage. "Well? What are all of you waiting for?"

Cherry sensed that these three young men intended to keep watch on Purdy's house throughout the night. He must not be given a chance to slip away a second time.

"Go home!" said Purdy. "Thank you very much. Good night!"

They made a show of removing themselves and their vehicles from his premises. Purdy went into the house and closed and bolted the door.

"He knows," Reed muttered to Cherry, a few minutes later, from the orchard, where they watched. Against the drawn curtains they saw Purdy's shadow, as he peered out into the night. "One of us had better be posted across the road at the lake," Reed said.

"What if he does guess he's under surveillance?" Cherry murmured. "What worries me is that Mac Cook passed us just now in the road." And she told Reed what had happened.

"That's not so good," Reed admitted. "If Purdy recognized Mac, the game is up."

Reed would not let her stay to keep watch. Cherry trudged back to camp alone. She considered walking over to the Eplers' or telephoning, to warn them. But suppose Purdy listened in on the party line, or glimpsed her moving toward the Eplers'? No, she had better be discreet and stay in camp.

Since Dr. Lowell did not need her at the infirmary, and most of the camp was asleep by now, Cherry went to bed, too. There she lay listening to the wind in the trees, and speculating whether Purdy would try to return to Tall Man's Island for whatever he had been doing there, or left there. Cherry thought of Reed and his two counselors keeping watch. The night had grown cloudy. A light rain started to fall. She hoped all would go well with Reed this night.

CHAPTER XII

Pursuit

"GUESS WHAT?" SAID SUE, POKING HER HEAD IN at the open cabin windows before Cherry was fully awake. "My cabin harvested the best vegetable crop at the Model Farm! We won the reward."

"Congratulations." Cherry yawned in spite of herself. "What reward? But first tell me, how did Katy do?"

"We call her Katy the Carrot Queen. Confidentially, Katy did some of the meanest jobs," Sue said. "You know, after you pull new carrots and beets, somebody has to take them down to the stream and wash off the tops and roots. And that somebody always gets wet and dirty. Well, Katy never squawked once. I *never* saw such a change in a girl!"

"Congratulations twice." Cherry smiled at Sue; they understood each other. "Now what about the reward?"

"Well, we Mountaineers piled into Uncle Bob's car last evening and he drove us to the village, and treated us to ice cream. Way past bedtime. I mean, it's an honor, besides being fun."

"You mean the other kids were green with envy."

"Well, yes." Sue grinned. Then she grew thoughtful. "You want to know something else? I heard a crazy thing at the garage, last evening."

Garage . . . Something Fred Epler had said came dimly to Cherry's memory.

"The garageman said," Sue chattered on, "and believe me, he was hopping mad— Anyway, he said someone broke in and stole his portable acetylene torch from out of the garage, a couple of nights ago. He thinks the thief is up to something because—"

"What! Did you say acetylene torch?"

Cherry jumped off her cot and shook Sue by the shoulders.

"Say it again." Sue did. "Are you absolutely sure?"

"Yes, Miss Cherry! Ask Katy and Ding. They were with me. They heard the garageman, too."

"All right, Sue. I'm happy to take your word for it."

An acetylene torch would account for the sparks in the dusk, for the ether odor, for Purdy's burned foot.

"Remember someone broke into Mr. Purdy's barn?" Sue asked. "Do you think the same fellow broke into the garage? Hey, Miss Cherry, you aren't listening!"

The sparks she and Reed had seen shot *down* instead of up. But of course! An acetylene torch was used either to weld or to cut hard metals, and the shower of sparks fell downward as the blue flame bit into the metal. So Purdy had been welding or cutting something made of metal—

The box—the box whose imprint she had seen in the mud—it could be steel, couldn't it? And if he was carrying the torch too, he might have rested the box on the ground as he shifted his load. Purdy wouldn't very likely be welding anything onto it— no, he'd be trying to *open* the steel box.

Suddenly all the pieces of the puzzle fell into place. Cherry thought, "Why, I'll bet Purdy was trying to open a steel cashbox he stole from the loan company safe."

She remembered that the news accounts had been singularly reticent about what money had been taken, or in what form. A casual reader like herself would assume that the safe held loose bundles of bills, but now that she came to think about it, most safes had compartments which held drawers for documents and contained a *locked steel strongbox* for cash. Purdy could have snatched the locked steel box of cash and concealed it under his voluminous raincoat.

"I'll bet that's it, or very close to the truth!"

And Purdy must have secreted the steel box in his barn all these weeks, struggling to unlock it, unable to force the steel lid open—until, as a last resort, he'd stolen an acetylene torch! Was she guessing right? Cherry thought so, because Purdy had

left so promptly after stealing the torch—for an isolated spot where he thought he would not be observed at work.

Cherry threw on her clothes, skipping the usual morning shower in her haste, and ran out on an astonished Sue. Reed, Mac, and the Eplers had to hear about the missing acetylene torch at once. Reed first, because he was nearest. As she ran down the road to Purdy's place, Cherry wondered how far Mr. Purdy might have succeeded in burning a steel box open. How handy was he with heavy tools? He'd burned his foot. On the other hand, Purdy developed all his own photographs, built props, installed locks on his barn.

To her horror, on arriving at Purdy's house, she found his house door wide open and not a soul around. Purdy's car was still here. Cherry called, ran to the barn, rattled its locked door. No answer, no lights. She looked in vain for any Thunder Cliff vehicles, but they had gone. What had happened since she left here last night?

"I'd better phone Thunder Cliff and find out if Reed is there."

Cherry sped down the road to the Eplers' farm. She could telephone from there and at the same time alert Mac Cook and Fred Epler.

Vernie and Fred were at breakfast in the kitchen. Mac ran out just as Cherry rapped and came in.

"Come back!" she called. "It's me, I'm alone."

Fred and Vernie stared at her. She had not even said good morning. Mac sheepishly returned to the kitchen, carrying his coffee cup.

"Something's happened, Miss Cherry?"

"A great deal has happened. In the first place, how come you were out walking on the road last evening, Mac Cook?"

"I just *had* to stretch my legs. It was dark. Didn't you see me wave to you? You didn't wave back."

"I saw you," said Cherry. "Purdy saw you, too. Purdy was driving with me."

"Purdy!" Mac leaned weakly against the wall. Vernie murmured that they had warned Mac against going out.

"We brought Purdy back." Cherry rapidly explained what had happened on their so-called picnic to Tall Man's Island. Then she repeated Sue's report about how and when the acetylene torch had been stolen. "Guess who stole it, and why," Cherry said dryly.

The Eplers and Mac were stunned. "The new steel cashbox," Mac muttered. "That's what he took from the safe—I knew it, I knew it! He needed the torch because the box has a combination lock that couldn't possibly be jimmied open."

"Where's Purdy now?" Fred Epler asked. "Let's be practical. What's our next move?"

"Let me call up Reed," said Cherry. "He was on night watch, but—"

Mac went with her into the hall to the telephone. She asked the operator for Thunder Cliff, waited to be put through, waited again while Reed was summoned from morning assembly to the telephone.

"Reed? . . . Cherry. I've just been over to Purdy's place and I don't understand—"

"All right, Cherry, take it easy. We had some bad luck, that's all. I'm glad you phoned. I tried to get you earlier but the line was busy."

"Reed, I don't mean to scold you, but where is Purdy?"

There was a pause, then Reed said:

"I don't know. The other two fellows wouldn't stay after two A.M., in the rain, with no satisfactory explanation from me. Of course I stayed on. But, well, I didn't fall asleep, I did watch, but somehow Purdy outfoxed me. He knows every inch of his place, and I—well—"

"Oh, Reed. Hold on—" Cherry muttered to Mac Cook what Reed had just said. Mac's face turned as gray as the wallpaper.

"Reed? Anything else?"

"Yes. Remember we left the canoe and the rowboat last evening at the shore just outside camp? Well, I checked, and the rowboat is gone. It couldn't have floated away. Purdy must have taken it. Sure as anything he's on his way back to Tall Man's Island—"

"—to get the money he left there. Of course. That's where he's gone." She felt Mac pulling at her arm.

"Call the police," said Mac urgently.

"What? Reed—you still there? . . . Mac wants to call the police. Can you come over here right away?"

Reed reminded her that today it was his job to take both the brother and sister camps into town to the circus. Although counselors would help, it was Reed's responsibility. He could not possibly get off. It would be an all-day project.

"I'm sorry, Cherry, but I have a job to do."

"You've been a tremendous help already," Cherry said warmly. "Thanks a million. I hope you'll sleep through the circus."

"So do I, for once. Good luck," Reed said, and hung up.

Cherry turned back to Mac Cook.

"From here on in," Mac said, "it's a race between us and Purdy for the stolen money—that is, for the proof. If Purdy makes off with it, I'll never be cleared!"

"But, Mac, you didn't *want* to call the police—"

"I do now! We need their help! Don't you see? Purdy has incriminated himself, a little, by stealing the acetylene torch. The garageman told Fred that Purdy wanted it awful badly; he'd been asking for it for days—" Mac took the phone out of Cherry's hands. His own hands trembled. "I'll call the police myself."

Cherry did not stay to hear what Mac would say. She went back to the kitchen to ask Vernie for a bite of breakfast. Considering what the next few hours could bring, she would need some nourishment. She remembered to telephone Dr. Lowell to ask for time off. He answered kindly, saying that since the entire camp, except for a few staff members, was going to the circus, Cherry could take as much time as she needed.

"Just be back by suppertime because Jan and I

expect some upset stomachs from too much hot dogs and popcorn."

She had barely hung up when a siren wailed somewhere down the road. It rapidly came nearer. In minutes the car which had once frightened Mac Cook away pulled into the Eplers' yard. Mac and Fred went out together to speak to Sergeant Braun of the state police. Two troopers, armed, were with him.

CHAPTER XIII

Tall Man's Island

~~~~~~

SERGEANT BRAUN WAS A BIG MAN IN A SMART UNI-
form, an older man, who knew this country well.
Cherry saw at once that he and his two officers who
had come so swiftly would be more than a match
for a city man like Purdy, even in the wooded fast-
ness of Tall Man's Island.

But finding Purdy was not the main problem.
Even finding the steel box and the money was not
enough. What they must do, said Sergeant Braun
after Mac and Fred explained the situation to him,
was to take Purdy *together with* the box and money,
which was evidence. Failing that (for Purdy might
be desperate enough to throw box and money into
the deep water currents around Tall Man's Island),
they must somehow draw from Purdy a statement
of his guilt.

Sergeant Braun paused in his explanation and
asked to use the telephone. Vernie showed him

where it was, and presently Cherry heard his clipped words instructing someone to "get it on the trailer and get it over here. On the double!"

Cherry wondered what piece of equipment Braun had sent for, but he didn't enlighten them. Instead, he continued with the line of thought which had been interrupted by his phone call.

"He won't be in any hurry to confess," the sergeant said. "He surely won't talk if he sees police around. I figure it's going to be up to somebody else."

He eyed Mac Cook speculatively, as if in doubt about him. Then the trooper considered Cherry.

"I believe we'll need you, Miss Ames," he said. "And you, Cook. Maybe this photographer fellow will be so provoked to see you that he will blurt out something."

Fred Epler volunteered to go along to the island. But Sergeant Braun said he'd rather Epler stayed with one of the two other troopers in the vicinity of Purdy's house and barn.

"He might grab his car and try to make a getaway. First, we'll check the barn."

At Sergeant Braun's order the two troopers went to Purdy's place to search the house, garage, and barn. They would break locks if necessary.

After a short wait, Trooper Miller returned. "We made a quick search, sir. Nothing of interest in Purdy's house or garage. All we found in the barn was a lot of old costumes and junk furniture. Wilkes stayed there."

"Right. The interesting stuff is on Tall Man's Island, then."

"Hadn't we better hurry up?" Mac asked anxiously.

"We'll go soon enough," Sergeant Braun told him, "and you watch your step, Cook. Remember you're wanted for robbery. Until Purdy confesses, you're still suspect."

Mac looked miserably at his brother and sister-in-law and Cherry. None of them could speak encouragement to him, not with any honesty.

"All right, Epler. Take up your post with Wilkes on Purdy's premises. Keep well out of sight. Oh, but first, let us borrow a shovel."

Fred got the shovel, then went off, obviously against Vernie's wishes. Sergeant Braun led Cherry, Mac, and the other trooper, Miller, down to the lake and through the wide margin of greenery at its edge. Then Cherry knew what he'd telephoned for.

A speedboat and driver in plain clothes were waiting there. Cherry had never seen the boat before, nor had Mac, judging by his expression.

"She can make thirty, thirty-five miles an hour or better," Sergeant Braun said. "Purdy is rowing, he's got a bad foot, and it was still raining early this morning. Made it too dim to see . . . Fog lying on the lake. Purdy wouldn't have dared to start until about six, more likely seven. I figure we'll still beat him to the island."

Once in the speedboat, they started off with a lurch which nearly threw Cherry into the water. The boat cut across the water like a knife, hurled at a speed which put Camp Blue Water in back of them in seconds. Camp Thunder Cliff seemed to streak past. Spray rose up so furiously that their garments got damp, and Cherry's hair whipped across her face.

Before long, up ahead, they saw a lone gray figure rowing along.

"Orders, sir?" called the driver.

"Bypass him!" Sergeant Braun called back. "Let's surprise him if we can." The sergeant motioned Cherry and Mac to crouch, as he did himself, so that Purdy would not recognize any of them as they swept past.

One minute, and they roared past the plodding rowboat. The driver took care, as Tall Man's Island hove into view, to keep going, to feint as if the noisy speedboat had some other destination.

But once around the island's curve, the driver cut the boat's speed, thus reducing the motor sound to a quiet put-put. Cherry directed him up to the island shore a bit farther than the spot where Purdy had moored his rowboat yesterday—and might, with luck, moor it again today. They secured the speedboat and climbed out.

Now their search began. Sergeant Braun ordered the driver of the speedboat to stay in the boat, out of sight under spreading branches, and keep an eye on the man in the rowboat. That was in case Purdy should try to escape or bypass them on the water.

"All right, miss. Show us what you found."

Cherry led Sergeant Braun, Trooper Miller, and Mac Cook to the area where, last evening, Purdy had been hiding. She showed them also the remains of the doused fire, and then, close to the shore line, the place of the sparks.

"All right," said Sergeant Braun. "Be quick and be quiet. Purdy will be here in a few minutes."

All of them started a close search. Cherry poked deep into the bushes where Purdy's hand had shown. She could not see anything but she nearly cut her own hand on a sharp, jagged edge.

"Sergeant Braun! I think I've found something!"

"Don't disturb any fingerprints, anybody," Braun cautioned.

The sergeant pulled a large, clean handkerchief out of his pocket, parted the bushes down to their roots, bent over, and came up with a crumpled steel box. Part of the lid and side was torn or, rather, burned away.

"Here it is," Sergeant Braun said with satisfaction. "The cashbox. Notice how the combination lock still holds?"

Punctured in several places, and badly battered, the reinforced steel box showed how hard Purdy must have worked over it. Cherry figured that he must have finished the job only shortly before she and Reed arrived last night, and had made a fire to prepare his supper when they surprised him. What had he intended to do next? And would it still matter now?

The steel box was empty.

Mac looked up at it. He was kneeling on the ground, struggling to reach his arm inside a large

"Sergeant Braun! I think I've found something!"

hollow log. Grunting that the log had been masked with freshly broken branches, Mac rolled flat on the ground, poking into it.

"I think he's shoved the torch in here," Mac panted. "You want to take over, Miller?"

Three minutes' probing, and out came the acetylene torch. Miller said he recognized it as belonging to the village garage. Purdy, in his ignorance of tools, had all but wrecked it.

But where was the cash? Cherry recalled the giant tree where Reed had noticed freshly turned earth. She showed the place to Trooper Miller. He dug, to no avail. They searched in the bushes and among roots of trees. Miller climbed several trees whose trunk and branches could form a cradle for a bundle. But they did not find anything.

"Maybe Purdy carried the money away on his person last night," Sergeant Braun suggested.

"I doubt it," Cherry said. "Dr. Lowell examined him at the infirmary, and I'm sure he would have noticed."

"Well, then," the trooper said, "here's how we'll handle this. I want you, Miss Ames, and you, Cook—" For several minutes Sergeant Braun outlined his plans as to what part each should play.

Suddenly Mac said, "I hear Pep landing!"

Sergeant Braun motioned for silence. He signaled Miller to take the steel box and the acetylene torch, using handkerchiefs. Then he motioned Cherry and Mac to stay but conceal themselves, where they were. They knew what they had to do. He and

Miller withdrew some yards behind them, out of sight and with guns drawn.

Cherry's knees were so shaky that she sat down on the log. A glance at Mac made her put aside her own fear. The whole of his future was at stake, depending on what Purdy did next—and Purdy was an exceedingly clever man. Mac tried to smile at her as they heard the man's steps coming through the crackling underbrush. From behind a screen of leaves they could see but not be seen.

Purdy emerged into full view. He carried a small overnight case and the by now familiar raincoat. Heading perilously close to the log where Cherry sat, Purdy moved past her to a giant tree and on to a patch of tall grass. There he put his suitcase and raincoat. Cherry, watching him, scarcely dared breathe.

Purdy tugged at a rock. It gave, and he burrowed. Apparently an animal had dug an underground lair there. In a few seconds Purdy's hands were full of bundles of green bills. A sharp snap of the suitcase's locks—

"I see you, Purdy!" Mac shouted. His fear was gone, and he was furiously angry.

Mac came bounding out of his hiding place, and, as he pushed aside the branches, exposed Cherry. She jumped to her feet.

Purdy was so astounded he stood stock-still. His eyes moved slowly from Mac to Cherry, back to Mac again. Though he changed color, Purdy did not lose his composure. Cherry stood there, fasci-

nated. For the first time she saw Mac Cook and
Purdy together, and saw that they were exactly the
same height. Yes, the raincoat, the mask, a hat
pulled low, the phrase, "Great balls of fire!" and in
a dim hall who would not mistake one man for the
other?

"Well! So it's Jack Waldron. I am not surprised,"
said Purdy calmly, sardonically. "When I saw you
on the road last night, I figured you had come for
your share of the take. What have you done to your
hair? It looks ridiculous!"

"Never mind my hair! And I'm not here to profit
by what you've—"

"Now listen to me, Jack. The deed is done. The
money is here. It's too bad you're blamed for it, but
if you had been smart enough to come in with me
in the first place— Remember I asked you?"

Mac shouted that he didn't want "anything to do
with stolen money—then or now!"

"You're a fool," Purdy said scornfully. "Be reasonable. I'll give you half the money, you'll serve a
short sentence—after all, *I* took the risks of doing
the job! Then, after that, you'll be a free man, and
pretty well heeled, too." Purdy added slyly, "Isn't
this arrangement what you wanted all along? Only
you left the initiative up to me?"

Cherry realized with a start that Purdy might to
some degree frame Mac yet. "Stop lying!" she exclaimed. "You can't drag Mac—Waldron—into a
crime you did alone."

"And what's it to you?" Purdy stared boldly at
Cherry. It was clear that possession of the money

made him cocky. "Ah, I see how it is. You are my little neighbor who kept watch on my movements— I daresay it was *you* who raided my barn? Then you reported to Jack Waldron. You have a little plan? But"—Purdy's voice grew deadly—"neither of you is as smart as you think you are."

Mac was in a rage, and incoherent. But Cherry knew she had to keep her head. She wondered anxiously why Braun and Miller did not close in. What were they waiting for?

"Come now, Jack, and you, too, Miss Nurse," Purdy went on. "Somehow I can never quite remember your name— How would you like, say, a thousand dollars apiece? To help you forget you have seen me here."

Cherry was all for playing along with him and pretending, for safety's sake, to accept the bribe. But Mac, who was still not formally cleared, would not even pretend.

"Two thousand," said Purdy. "No? Then how much, Jack?"

"Not at any price. I've told you that before."

Purdy put his hands in his pockets. "That is really too bad. If you'd make a reasonable deal with me, I could let you go. I could afford to be generous— but you both are fools. As it is"—Purdy's face was evil—"you'll never live to tell the story."

He drew a revolver from his pocket.

"You—you don't dare use that," Mac said. "You don't want to be charged with murder, do you?"

Faintly, almost as if she were imagining it, Cherry heard the slightest of leaf sounds behind her. She hoped it was Braun and Miller. It *had* to be. She and Mac could not wait many minutes longer. Not with that gun cocked in Purdy's hand.

"Of course I would use it," Purdy said to Mac. "As for a murder charge, I can leave the country immediately. It will take time to find your bodies on this island—or, if I choose, by dragging Long Lake"

"You'd be caught," said Cherry.

She was certain about the sounds now. The two men *were* inching forward. But where she stood, she could be caught in cross fire. The state police officers must know this, they must be trying to avoid gunfire on either side—

"I am bored with arguing with you," said Purdy. He lovingly patted the suitcase. "And who says it is murder? I could quite easily plead self-defense. And—"

Without warning, Miller sneaked up behind Purdy and seized him. Purdy tilted backward, completely taken by surprise.

"Drop that gun!"

With Miller's arms like a vise around him, and Braun now in front of him holding a gun, Purdy had no choice, Cherry thought, but to drop his revolver.

Instead, Purdy fired.

The shot went wild, digging into the earth. Sergeant Braun remarked, "You want that money awful badly, don't you, Purdy?"

The sergeant ordered Miller to put handcuffs on Purdy, then he turned around to speak to Mac.

"I think you're in the clear now, son, and you can thank your nurse friend for it. All right, now, Purdy. We'll take you back to my office. You can make your statement there."

Purdy was beaten enough to make his confession in the boat. Riding back to the village at an easier speed, Cherry and Mac Cook heard what he had to say.

Purdy had been doing fairly well with his photography studio in New York City until a certain loan company bought the building where Purdy's studio was located. They raised the rent to a figure he could not afford. Purdy was forced to move. In a crowded city he had a long, hard search to find a desirable location, and he never again did as well with his photography business. Some clients forgot him, and others simply would not seek him out at the new address. Only a few old customers came back. Purdy was failing. He felt that the loan company had ruined him. And he was vengeful.

Purdy conceived a plan whereby he thought he could kill two birds with one stone—if he could steal from the loan company! That, in his distorted mind, would even the score, and restore his failing business. He needed a great deal of money. For even his country cottage, in these Pennsylvania mountains, was mortgaged and he was in danger of losing that too—a fact that nobody suspected. Purdy's plan to rob the loan company and pay his debts grew into an obsession.

Purdy went to the loan company's main office and "cased the joint"—that is, he learned the physical layout of the place, and where the cash was kept. In order to have an excuse to visit the office frequently, and learn all he needed to know, Purdy applied for a small loan. This the company reluctantly granted. Among other things Purdy observed during his visits were the loan company employees. He saw Jack Waldron—or Mac Cook—although he never spoke to this particular cashier.

It was a stroke of luck for Purdy to meet Jack Waldron—or Mac Cook—in the modest New York City restaurant where both ate their suppers. First, Purdy made very sure that Mac, who dealt with large numbers of clients, did not recognize him. Second, Purdy took care not to reveal his full name and address to Mac. He went to work to gain the young man's friendship and confidence. Mac was lonely; it was easy.

In this way, during many evenings while they ate together, Purdy drew out from the unsuspecting Mac such information as where the bulk of the cash was kept, on what dates most clients came to make payments on their loans, and the habits of the staff people and the two women who had charge of the safe. Specifically, he learned that one always attended an afternoon executive meeting on the fifteenth and thirtieth of the month, or on the Friday preceding if these dates fell on Saturday or Sunday. He learned that the other woman usually took a break to powder her nose between four forty and four fifty. Thus Purdy knew the safe, open to receive clients' payments, would be left unguarded for about ten minutes.

After learning this, Purdy made his proposal to Mac. When Mac refused, Purdy laughed it off—and thought he had nothing further to fear from Mac. He knew, of course, about Mac's vacation plans; it gave him a perfect setup to impersonate Mac during the robbery and thus frame him.

The only flaw in Purdy's plan was that he had expected the immense sums of cash to be lying loose in the compartments of the safe. Instead, the compartments held only papers. He figured, correctly, that the money he sought was in the locked steel box in the upper-right compartment. This he took.

Unluckily for Purdy, when he carried the locked steel box back to his studio, he was unable to force open the combination lock. He cursed the stubborn, heavy metal chest when his efforts to pierce the reinforced steel with other tools proved futile.

News of the robbery broke in the papers, and though Purdy, anxiously reading four or five newspapers every day, did not see his name mentioned, still he began to feel afraid. At his wit's end about how to open the box, and running short of money, he fled to his cottage in Pennsylvania. Here, at least, he felt he could work, unobserved and in less haste, on the box. He stored it in his locked barn. He had no idea that Mac Cook was in the neighborhood, nor that a quick-witted nurse at Camp Blue Water had caught on to the fact that something was afoot. He threw the mask into the lake, although he realized afterward that he could more easily have buried or burned it.

He tried every means he could think of, every

tool he could find or borrow, to open the box. When his barn was broken into, and the precious box jeopardized, he was afraid to report the attempted burglary to the police. Purdy had puzzled a great deal over who had broken in, and why, but he never seriously considered that someone in the neighborhood knew what his barn really held.

So he had gone ahead, conceited by nature, made still more cocky by his success in stealing the box. He had discounted Mac Cook as having enough spirit to try to clear himself. But Purdy had figured wrong. As she stepped out of the boat at the camp dock, Cherry reminded Sergeant Braun that the mask was in the Blue Water safe.

"Right," he said. "We'll pick it up this afternoon. Maybe you'd better warn the Wrights to expect us; they might be a bit surprised to see the police walk in."

Cherry promised to tell them, and smiled to herself as she thought, "But not one half as surprised as they will be when they find we had a criminal's mask on our Can-You-Name-This Shelf!"

CHAPTER XIV

Events Week

ALMOST BEFORE ANYONE REALIZED, IT WAS THE LAST week of August and the closing week of camp. Everyone was sorry but terrifically busy and excited about the grand climax of the summer: Events Week. A bittersweet kind of feeling . . .

In the gala goings-on, Cherry did not like to mention anything so out of key as the Purdy affair. She talked about it only to the Wrights and to Reed Champion. Reed dropped in at Blue Water daily during this last week, partly to see about the water pageant and the final brother-sister party, but mostly to visit Cherry.

"I still want to look at you and see with my own eyes that you're unscathed," Reed said. "I never before met a girl who'd go through such a hair-raising adventure, and bob up smiling."

"A nurse has to be resourceful, you know," said Cherry, with an almost straight face.

"Well, let me tell you, I never saw one bit of that circus! I kept wishing I was on Tall Man's Island."

Reed and Cherry smiled at each other, and by mutual consent talked instead about this exciting last week of camp. Reed, an old-time camper, advised Cherry to brace herself for practically a week-long festival.

The keenest excitement was brought on by the awards. Even before Aunt Bet announced them at a Special Assembly in the Playhouse, the awards caused a wave of rumors and some secret, quite unnecessary tears, mopped up by Nurses Jan and Cherry. Nobody was surprised when Katy Osborn won the Camp Blue Water medal for general improvement. What made it extra nice, though, was Lil Baker's telling in Assembly how, when she proposed Katy's name, every girl in the Mountaineers cabin voted yes. "They bunked with Katy—they ought to know." Katy was so moved she burst into tears all over Sue's shoulder. Sue had to extricate herself in order to go up on the platform to receive her own award. The Intermediates had voted Sue the best all-around camper in their group.

Ding shared gardening awards with one senior and three Midgets. Mary Alice received public notice for her cookies, baked on rainy days only. Katy won a dramatics commendation for her Juliet. And Sue, along with every girl whom Mac Cook had taught, won honorable mention for their dolls made of pine cones and driftwood and gnarled roots. Cherry was so excited about the awards that she admitted to Aunt Bet, "I wish I'd won something myself."

"I think you did," Aunt Bet said. "Isn't clearing an innocent man quite a reward?"

Next, the girls and their counselors turned the Playhouse into a regular fair, heaped with the lovely and interesting things they had collected and made and grown during the summer. Many parents came especially to see their daughters' fine "handmade originals": handmade sewing baskets and bread baskets, bright-colored mobiles, wooden buttons and brooches and book ends. One wall was hung with new finger paintings, pencil sketches, and photographs, although Mr. Purdy was mysteriously not on hand to judge, this time. Cherry's Can-You-Name-This Shelf contributed a fine collection of unusual growing plants, and Katy brought several varieties of delicate pressed ferns as a gift from her cabin. Heaps of luscious vegetables and bouquets of flowers testified to the girls' harvest at the Model Farm.

The only thing not on exhibit were the Midgets' ducklings which had grown so plump that Uncle Bob proposed, "Let's ask Sophie to roast them and we'll all enjoy a fine duck dinner." The Midgets were brokenhearted at the idea, and Uncle Bob had a hard time to convince them that he was only joking. Another character besides the ducklings who had grown up during the summer was Katy's kitten, now long-legged and almost a cat. Vernie Epler had fallen in love with the gentle little gray creature, and since Katy's mother was not hospitable to pets,

Vernie was going to adopt her. Mac Cook, too, was being adopted in a sense, but Cherry was waiting for him to come back from testifying in New York. At the big brother-sister party, Mac could tell his own good news.

First came the water pageant. Blue Water and Thunder Cliff had been preparing their floats, tableaux, music, and swimming formations for the past two weeks. Not everyone was skilled enough to take part—besides, someone had to be the audience.

The day of the water pageant, the last Friday, arrived all blue sky, sunshine, and calm blue water. Perfect! Along the leafy shores of the lake, young people, their counselors, and parents found comfortable places to watch. Now at the end of August, in the afternoon, the mountain air was turning cooler. Brisk breezes blew the leaves wrong side out, their undersides showing silver, like thousands of banners.

Unless an onlooker knew that each float was based on a rowboat, he would have wondered how even the powerful swimmers—senior boys—swung the spectacles slowly, smoothly along. The band led the pageant, in two bunting-decorated boats, and Cherry saw D. V. tootling away for all he was worth. The Midgets, with the ducklings swimming alongside, came next. Intermediate boys offered a glee club, their voices ringing out over the water. The Ding-dong Bells floated past, costumed as flowers. There were floats of water nymphs and fierce pirates, Greek gods and gauzy ballet girls to admire, and a boatload of clowns to laugh at. Finally the chorus of senior boys and girls closed the floating pageant.

Everyone returned to Camp Blue Water where boxed lunches of fried chicken and mounds of ice-cold watermelons awaited them on the grass.

"Sophie has done herself proud," someone said.

"I think Mac Cook is helping her. It's good to have him back."

Cherry looked around for Mac. He had promised her he would try to be back in time for the big party, and he was! He came out of the Mess Hall, smooth-shaven, his hair now mostly a natural brown, smiling shyly and looking younger and happier than Cherry had ever seen him. The kids nearly upset his big platter of bread and butter, as they crowded around him.

"Mac! That doll you showed me how to make —it won an award!"

"Where have you been, Mac? Didn't you like us any more?"

"Mac, you look so different," Sue shrilled, "and so nice! Better, I mean."

"I feel better, honey."

Mac smiled at Cherry, at the Wrights, and went on to pass the platter, with a troop of children at his heels. Aunt Bet nodded quietly at Cherry. It had been agreed, earlier at a meeting in the Main House among the Wrights, the Eplers, the Clemences, Cherry, and Reed, that there was no need to announce the entire story to the camps. Anyone who was interested could read in the newspapers of Purdy's guilt and Mac's innocence. Mac Cook—or Jack Waldron—was now completely cleared. The

newspapers, like Sergeant Braun, gave full credit
to the good work done by Cherry Ames. As for Mac
himself, he only wanted to forget the whole thing.

Presently he came over to where Cherry and Reed
were eating their supper together. Mac sat down
beside them under the tree.

"I suppose Fred told you?"

"That the loan company offered you your job
back?" Cherry said. "That's good news."

"No, better than that. Fred wants me to have a
half share in the farm." Mac's face actually glowed.
"Fred says he means it, he thinks it never was fair
that I was placed in the orphanage. You know what?
I used to dream about this farm all the time I was
growing up."

Cherry was so pleased she could only gulp. Reed
asked:

"Will Fred's farm support three of you?"

"We don't know yet. It probably will in time. In
the meantime, the Clemences asked me to come
back and take care of their greenhouse. Pretty nice
people."

"It looks as if your lonely days are over, Mac."

"That's right. Now I have a family—as well as
a farm!"

No one mentioned Purdy. Though they were
all thinking about him, there was nothing anyone
could say. Someone teased Uncle Bob by telling
him, "Now you can loaf for the other ten months
of the year, can't you?" He nearly exploded, ex-
plaining that camp work kept him and Aunt Bet
busy the year round.

The long afternoon grew dusky, the first stars appeared. By the time the smallest of the boys were boosted into the truck and station wagons, and the older boys had taken the boats back to Thunder Cliff, evening had come. Reed, dashing past Cherry, paused for a moment to show her a shooting star.

"Make a wish on it," Cherry said.

"I wish for us to meet again." Reed smiled down at her.

"That's easy. We will."

The girl campers, tired and happy, went to their cabins. Tomorrow they would complete their packing. Tomorrow they would take the afternoon train.

"Give me your address, Miss Cherry," said Sue, "and I'll write to you faithfully."

"Misspelled, no doubt. Oops, I'm sorry," said Katy. "I forgot." Katy had a brand-new grin and a new self-reliance. "Will you come to the camp reunion at Thanksgiving, Miss Cherry? Lil and our whole cabin will be there."

"If I'm not the nurse with a traveling circus or something like that, I'll surely be there," Cherry promised.

She said good night and crossed the path to her own cabin. In the field the privileged seniors were having a last, sentimental campfire, a last evening sing. She entered her counselors' cabin to find Leona Jackson standing gingerly on a bed.

"It's that field mouse," Leona squeaked. "I swear it's the same one. He knows we're moving out, and he's moved back in!"

Cherry and Ruth J. persuaded Leona that there

was room enough in the cabin for them all. They should have packed, or gone right to bed after this long, stirring day, but everyone wanted to sit up and talk. Finally, after Lights Out, Cherry stole out onto the step for one more look at lake and hills and stars.

"What a lovely summer it has been!"

She remembered a fawn she had seen this summer running in the woods, its dappled coat dappled again by shadows of leaves. She breathed in again the cool woodsy fragrance to which she had fallen asleep and awakened. And the wonderful people! It had been a rich experience getting to know all of them. Sue—who wasn't unlike Cherry at twelve —and Katy who had put up a game fight and won it, the darling Lowells and Wrights, Fred and Vernie, and, above all, Mac.

Yes, it had been quite a summer! Smiling to herself, Cherry went contentedly into the cabin. This summer had rested and refreshed her. She was all ready for a new adventure.